DISNEP · PIXAR

ONWARD

The Search for the PHOENIX GEM

An In-Questigation

Printed in the United States of America

First Hardcover Edition, February 2020

1 3 5 7 9 10 8 6 4 2

FAC-020093-19354

Library of Congress Control Number: 2019948119

ISBN 978-1-368-05210-8

Visit disneybooks.com

SUSTAINABLE FORESTRY INITIATIVE   Certified Sourcing
www.sfiprogram.org
SFI-00993

Logo Applies to Text Stock Only

DISNEY · PIXAR

ONWARD

The Search for the PHOENIX GEM

An In-Questigation

By Steve Behling

DISNEY PRESS

Los Angeles • New York

Chapter 1

It. Was. Bonkers. *ABSOLUTELY BONKERS.*

Those were the only words Sadalia could think of to describe what had happened that day at New Mushroomton High School.

Sadalia Brushthorn was a sophomore, and she had a full course load. She was taking Alchemy, Realm History, and lots of other stuff that didn't really hold her interest. But then there was journalism.

Journalism was her favorite. She had a nose for news. At least, that's what her father said. He said she had the ears for it, too. "Elves like us have a keen sense of hearing. That'll make you the best reporter to get the inside scoop!"

Sadalia's hearing seemed average to her, but one thing of which she was certainly certain (she liked to say that a lot—"certainly certain") was that she would have a career as a reporter one day. Even when she had been no bigger than a gnome, she had always asked, "Who? What? Where? When? Why?" and not necessarily in that order.

In fact, she already was a reporter, and she considered herself to be a pretty darn good one, too. In addition to honing her writing skills in her journalism class, Sadalia was a reporter for the school newspaper, *The Fortnightly Dragon*. It was considered to be biweekly, which implied that the newspaper came out once every two weeks, but for reasons she didn't really understand, the paper came out three times a week.

When Sadalia asked the journalism teacher, Mrs. Nightdale, why that was, she laughed and said, "Who knows? It's a mystery, wrapped in an enigma, then placed inside a conundrum and baked in an oven at three hundred and fifty degrees for thirty-five minutes. We're certainly *hot* off the presses here at *The Fortnightly Dragon*!"

Sadalia had no idea what any of that meant.

But she wasn't complaining. More newspaper issues meant more writing opportunities. No one in her journalism class had volunteered more often or pitched more ideas than Sadalia. She was constantly looking for a story that would be her big break, one that would prove to everyone that she had what it took to be an honest-to-goodness newspaper reporter.

But most of the stuff that happened at school fell into one of two categories: boring, or really, really boring. Sadalia didn't want to waste her time writing stories about the latest happenings of the Friends of the Unicorn Club (boring—plus, everyone knew unicorns were the most disgusting things in the realm), or interviewing the guy who fixed the drinking fountains (really, really boring). It didn't help that not many exciting things went on in the quiet suburbs of New Mushroomton. But someone had to cover those things, to be sure, and it was usually her.

She just wanted that one big story—the one that would change her life forever.

Then one day, she got exactly what she wanted. And her life was never the same.

✦ ◈ ✦

It had started out as an ordinary weekend evening. Sadalia and her friends were hanging out, walking near the high school right before sunset. There was some commotion in the form of police activity near the old town fountain, which wasn't entirely unusual. But what came next was *extremely* unusual.

Where everything had been normal, suddenly a swirl of red smoky mist appeared in the air just above the ground. It flowed like ink through water, snaking around their feet and legs, heading right for the school. The mist began to gather, creating a sphere. Then tendrils formed, extending from the sphere almost like tentacles. The tentacles writhed and burst through the windows, doors, and even the walls of the school!

Sadalia's friends' immediate reactions were to run and hide. But Sadalia's was different.

She started to race forward, heading right for the school. She would've kept going, too, if one of her friends hadn't pulled her back.

"What are you doing?" Althea screamed. "You'll be killed! Or worse!"

Sadalia wasn't sure what was worse than being killed. But she didn't need her reporter's instincts to tell her that something HUGE was happening, and she had a front-row seat.

Althea yanked Sadalia behind a row of shrubs. While her friends ducked and kept their heads down, Sadalia peered through some branches to watch the action.

That's when she saw the smoky tendrils grabbing bits and pieces of the school and the surrounding area: everything from walls to desks to lockers to cars. The smoke seemed to be forming a kind of structure, which Sadalia thought looked almost like a skeleton.

The debris gathered all around this skeleton, and the school roared to literal life as a massive dragon. She didn't know whether to laugh or scream when she saw that the monster had the face of the goofy dragon mascot that had been painted on one of the walls of the school's gymnasium. She had no idea how it was happening, or why it was happening. Nevertheless, it was unfolding right before her eyes.

"Barley, run!"

She heard the voice and recognized it as belonging to a kid from her class, Ian Lightfoot. He'd always seemed nice enough, but she didn't really know him all that well. In fact, her only interactions with him had been kind of strange. One time, she and her friends had been kicking a soccer ball around after school when it went flying toward Ian. Sadalia asked him to toss it back, but instead of doing that, he gently—and *gently* was an overstatement—rolled the ball toward her. It didn't even complete half the distance between them. Then he ran away.

And just the other day, Ian had invited Sadalia and her friends to his birthday party. There was going to be cake at the party; Ian was very

clear about that. But then his older brother, Barley, showed up in this beat-up purple van, and suddenly, Ian was all kinds of . . . embarrassed, maybe? Suddenly, there *was* no party. Ian said it was a "huge misunderstanding," as if inviting people to your house for a party could be a misunderstanding. Sadalia had also noticed that Ian had pen ink on his face, and after she pointed it out, he seemed to get even more embarrassed. He ran off right after that. The whole thing was pretty awkward.

But now Ian was calling out to his brother as the massive dragon took off in their direction. The beast was charging at Barley, who was obviously no match for a dragon. He'd be crushed for sure!

Sadalia saw that Barley had something in his hands, and it looked like the dragon wanted it. Barley raised his hand and hurled whatever he had been holding in the opposite direction. The dragon immediately lost interest in Barley and went chasing after the object.

This thing moves surprisingly fast for something

so big, Sadalia thought. In no time, the dragon had covered the distance between Barley and the thrown object. But when the dragon recovered whatever it was, it looked furious.

With glaring eyes, the dragon turned to face Barley once more. It was easy to see that it didn't appreciate being tricked. The dragon decided the best way to express its displeasure was to breathe a mouthful of fire in Barley's direction. The flames scorched the ground, keeping Ian and Barley separated.

Then the dragon hesitated for a moment as wings sprouted from the sides of its body. They started to flap, lifting the dragon into the sky. It was heading closer and closer to Ian and Barley, and Sadalia wasn't sure if she should keep looking or not.

But her reporter's instincts wouldn't allow her to turn away. Rather than run from danger, as most of the crowd was doing, Sadalia moved closer to it as she tried to get a better view. She thought she heard Althea shouting behind her, but her curiosity outweighed everything. And it was a good thing she stayed, otherwise she would have missed the Manticore.

Because apparently it was *that* kind of day.

Chapter 2

Sadalia noticed two things about the Manticore right away.

One: the Manticore was this weird bat, scorpion, lion creature. She looked like one of those mix-and-match games that include wild combinations of different heads, bodies, and tails. Sadalia didn't even know what to call the creature until a young centaur nearby pointed and shouted in awe, "It's the Manticore!" Sadalia made a note to herself to do more research later.

Two: the Manticore was carrying a massive sword. She came swooping in and swiped at the dragon. The power of the hit completely knocked the beast onto its side.

Squinting her eyes, Sadalia could see there was someone riding atop the Manticore. It was an elf woman, but Sadalia didn't recognize her. She wondered if this was the boys' mom.

The woman called out, "It's okay, boys! We'll take care of—"

Then the Manticore started wobbling midair, and the woman stopped saying whatever she had been trying to say.

Sadalia watched as Ian and Barley ran away from the dragon, along the path the fire had burned on the ground.

Suddenly, the Manticore flew toward the dragon and sliced at it again. There was something inside the beast that Sadalia could see now, but she couldn't quite make out what it was. She guessed it was something vital to the dragon's very survival.

While the battle raged, Sadalia noticed Ian and Barley at the top of a hill. Barley handed a long wooden staff to Ian. There appeared to be something bright and glowing at its tip, like a gem. Ian was saying something, but he was too far away and she couldn't make out the words.

Then a bright beam of light erupted from the gem atop the staff.

In the meantime, the dragon took flight and chased after the Manticore and her partner. They soared over the cliffs and the ocean and back around toward land. The Manticore dragged her sword along the ground, kicking up dirt into the dragon's eyes. While it was temporarily blinded, she swooped back around and sliced off the dragon's wings one by one.

Sadalia thought the Manticore could actually vanquish the beast until it reared up and swatted the Manticore right out of the sky. Both Manticore and rider plummeted toward the ground, landing hard.

The Manticore tried to move, but it looked as though she was in pain. She couldn't hold the sword anymore. So the woman who had been riding the Manticore picked it up.

Sadalia ran closer and watched the woman scamper up the dragon's tail, sword in hand. She showed no signs of slowing, nor would she let anything stop her. She charged right toward a glowing red light deep inside the creature.

The dragon seemed not to care about the woman in that moment, however. Its focus was once again on Ian and Barley. It reared up, ready to strike.

Then the woman cried out, this time with more conviction than Sadalia had ever heard from anyone before: "I AM A MIGHTY WARRIOR!" She stabbed the dragon, but only part of the sword made it past the monster's thick exterior. It froze.

"Hurry, I can't hold this for long!" the woman shouted. She stayed on the dragon's back, holding the sword with both hands. It was still stuck into the dragon, and she refused to let go.

In the distance, Sadalia could see that the gem from Ian's staff had started to spin, raising itself from the top of the staff. It glowed as the staff began shaking. Sadalia had an idea of what this was, but saying the word out loud seemed silly.

Could it be . . . *magic?*

But Sadalia couldn't keep watching Ian and Barley. The dragon had somehow pushed the sword out from its rocky hide! The dragon squirmed and bucked the woman off its back, and the sword flew into a pile of lockers that had been pulled from the high school.

"Boys! It's coming back!" the woman shouted.

The dragon seemed to be gathering its strength, ready to go on the attack once more. Ian had left his brother on the hill—and was now standing in midair! He called out, "Boom" (something or other), and fireworks exploded from the staff he held in his hands. The dragon was temporarily blinded!

It whirled its tail around, but Ian called out something else. This time Sadalia heard it: *"Aloft Elevar!"* And the dragon's tail stopped before it could strike him.

While Ian dealt with the dragon, Sadalia saw that the woman was trying to reach the sword in the pile of debris.

The dragon was furious now. It curled its tail,

whipping it around, and managed to dislodge the staff from Ian's hands, flinging it into the ocean. The invisible bridge upon which Ian had apparently been standing disappeared, and he fell to the ground. Sadalia swore she heard a crack when Ian's ankle hit.

The dragon returned its attention to Barley. When Sadalia looked back at Ian, she was surprised to see he was holding yet another staff in his hands! She wondered how he had pulled that off, realizing that everything she had believed in was being turned upside down right in front of her.

Then she heard Ian shout, "Voltar Thundersword!" Or was it "Thundershirt"? She had no idea what language he was speaking, but it was clearly an incantation of some sort.

A blinding flash of white lightning zigzagged from Ian's staff, blasting the dragon. Bits and pieces of the school flew everywhere, revealing the glowing red sphere embedded within the dragon's chest.

Sadalia looked for the woman once again and

heard her call, "Ian!" She had regained the sword, and now threw it toward the teenager. He caught the sword using magic, then sent it shooting toward the dragon's core.

The dragon rose once more, but Ian drove the sword into the beast's center. It instantly exploded! Debris flew in every direction, and Sadalia was blown back by the force of the blast.

When she got to her feet, the dragon was on the ground. Only it wasn't a dragon anymore. It was just the rubble of New Mushroomton High School.

Sadalia was still lost in the incredible moment when she felt someone grab her arm. "Sal! I've been talking to you for like the last five minutes!" Althea said. "I think it's safe to get out of here now!"

"Of course it's safe!" Sadalia exclaimed. "The dragon is gone."

"You don't know that," Althea replied. "Who knows what other monster might pop up!"

When they were farther away, Sadalia turned

and saw smoke and dust rising in the distance. She wondered if Ian and Barley were okay. In the chaos, she hadn't seen what happened to them or the Manticore and the elf woman. But all seemed quiet now.

"How did this happen?" she said to herself. "*Why* did this happen?"

She didn't know. But she was going to find out.

Chapter 3

It's not every day that your school turns into a dragon. In fact, it's not ANY day that your school turns into a dragon. Except this one day.

Sadalia was sitting on top of the biggest story that had ever happened, and she knew it. But what was she going to *do* about it?

Looking around, she saw vans had arrived from several TV stations. A stream of reporters was milling around with their camera and sound crews, each trying to work their way toward the battleground. Police were holding them back, but Sadalia's heart sank. *She* wanted to get the story, the scoop, the exclusive. How was she going to compete with all that?

"Sal! Hello? SAL!"

Sadalia's thoughts were broken by Althea waving her hand in front of her face. "What in

Marsalax's Beak was THAT?" Althea asked, arms raised over her head. She was swinging them around, indicating, well, everything. Althea was one of Sadalia's closest friends, but she *did* have a flair for dramatics. It came in handy for theater, and she would be performing one of the lead roles in the upcoming school play, *The Minotaur Cometh*. But it could become a little tiresome in real life.

"Well," Sadalia said slowly, "it appears our school turned into a dragon."

"Yeah, I know that!" Althea said. "But, like, what *was* it?"

"A dragon?" Sadalia said, hoping it was the right answer.

"No!" Althea said, shaking her head from side to side. "Someone was responsible for this! Remember that kid who was talking to us the other day? The one who invited us to the party then disinvited us?"

"Who, Ian?"

"Yeah, Ian! Is that his name? Anyway, I heard

that he's TOTALLY responsible for this mess. I could have guessed it. He seemed pretty shifty. I may be a cyclops, but my eye doesn't miss a thing."

"Involved, definitely," Sadalia said, her reporter's brain kicking in. "But responsible? We won't know that until we find out the facts."

"What are you, some kind of detective?"

"No, a reporter," Sadalia said. "Which is kind of the same thing, if you stop and think about it." Already, she was considering what Althea had said—that Ian was somehow responsible for everything that had happened. "Anyway. What else have you heard?"

"This one's pretty big. Since it was all Ian's fault, I heard he's going to be arrested. And then expelled," Althea said, her eye widening. "Or maybe expelled, then arrested. I'm not sure how that all works."

"They can't expel him!" Sadalia exclaimed. "*Or* arrest him! Either one! He saved everyone!"

"Maybe he set the whole thing up just so he could look like some kind of big hero," Althea said, shrugging her shoulders. "Maybe he just wanted some attention. Like when he invited us to his party."

Sadalia thought about that. It just didn't add up. Granted, she didn't know Ian that well. Actually, she didn't know him at all. That was something she was going to have to change if she wanted to get the story.

"Hello? Sadalia? Am I losing you again?" Althea said, waving a hand in front of the reporter's eyes.

Sadalia snapped to. "Sorry, I was just thinking. I don't buy that this was some kind of hoax. I think this really happened, and obviously Ian was involved in some way since he fought the dragon. But not as some kind of criminal mastermind."

"I guess we'll find out," Althea said, pointing into the distance. "The police are here now, talking with Principal Pipplemell."

Sadalia craned her head to look past her friend. She saw an officer talking to the principal, who had rushed over to the school when she received word of what happened.

"I gotta go. See ya later, Althea!" Sadalia said, sprinting for the police car.

"Where are you going?" Althea shouted.

"Where do you think? I've gotta get an interview with Principal Pipplemell!" Sadalia said, pointing to the gnome. "Before any of those TV stations do. This is MY story!"

But before she could go any farther, she found she had run into a thin line of yellow plastic ribbon. The ribbon stretched, and then she fell over, backward.

A satyr police officer walked over, offering her hand, but Sadalia got up on her own, dusting herself off. Her hands darted into her bag, and she pulled out a small pad of paper and a pencil.

"You should be more careful where you're going," the officer said. "That police tape is surprisingly strong."

"Yeah, I know," Sadalia said. "Thanks for the tip. Speaking of tips, what can you tell me about what happened here today, Officer . . ."

The officer leaned in, showing Sadalia her

badge. "Gore. And I'm not at liberty to discuss anything. Now, I suggest you get back to class."

Sadalia stared at the officer, then turned her head slowly, her gaze moving to the pile of rubble that moments ago had been a dragon, and a few moments before that had been New Mushroomton High School. She also didn't need to point out that it was the weekend. Her head swiveled back toward Officer Gore.

Gore sighed, realizing her mistake. "But that's probably not gonna happen any time soon, now that I think about it. So, I don't know, go home, maybe?"

"I can't go home. My name's Sadalia Brushthorn, and I'm a reporter for *The Fortnightly Dragon*, and—"

"That's the school paper, isn't it?" Officer Gore asked. "The one that comes out three times a week?"

Sadalia nodded. "Yes, exactly. So anyway—"

"Why doesn't it come out fortnightly? And

what is a fortnight, anyway? I never could figure that one out."

"Yeah, no one can," Sadalia said. "But it's not really important right now. What IS important is that I speak to Principal Pipplemell. She's standing right over there with that other police officer. Think you can let a reporter through?"

Officer Gore looked at Sadalia and smiled. "Nope."

"Look, I'm doing an article for the school paper about what just happened here. It's the scoop of the century, and I really need to talk to Principal Pipplemell now!"

"I'm sorry, but Officer Bronco said this whole area's off-limits. If I can't let those big-time TV reporters in, there's no way I can let you through. Besides, he's taking a couple folks into custody right now."

Sadalia looked over at the police car, and saw that both Ian and his brother, Barley, were now in the hands of the police!

Without another word, Sadalia ducked under

the yellow police tape. Officer Gore tried to stop her, but she was too fast. The officer's arms missed her completely, and she darted off toward the police cruiser in the distance.

The elf woman who had been with the Manticore during the fight was with Ian and Barley now. The police officer was talking to her, leaving the two teenagers by themselves for a moment. Principal Pipplemell was already gone.

Sadalia thought it was weird that the police would leave two suspects just hanging out by themselves, but she didn't have time to process it.

A moment later, she was up in Ian's face with her notepad. "Ian! I'm Sadalia, from *The Fortnightly Dragon*! And we're in the same science class, too. I'd like to ask you a few questions about the strange events of today."

"Uh, sure, I guess," Ian said, scratching his head. "I don't know if now's the best time, though—"

"It's definitely *not* the best time," said the centaur police officer. "How'd you get in here? I thought we'd set up a perimeter around this place!"

Officer Gore came running over, huffing and puffing. She stopped right next to Sadalia, then bent over, resting her hands on her thighs and breathing heavily. "Officer Bronco. Sorry about that. This one managed to, uh, slip through our defenses, despite our, uh, best efforts."

Officer Bronco raised an eyebrow. "Yeah, I can see you did everything you possibly could." Sadalia could have sworn there was a trace of a smile creeping out from under his thick mustache.

"Is it true that these two young individuals are going to be expelled-from-school-slash-arrested?" Sadalia asked, stepping closer to Officer Bronco.

"Is it . . . who are you, kid?" Officer Bronco asked.

"Sadalia Brushthorn. Reporter for *The Fortnightly Dragon*."

"Look, Sadalia, I'm sure you're a very good reporter, but we're not taking any questions right now, okay?" Officer Bronco said as he placed his hindquarters between her and the two boys.

"But—" Sadalia started to say before she felt Officer Gore guiding her away.

"You gotta come with me," Officer Gore said. "This is police business, Sadalia."

Sadalia turned to the police car and was dismayed to see Ian and Barley already inside. Officer Bronco shut the door. Then he and the mysterious woman got into the front of the vehicle and drove off.

"Whatever happened to innocent until proven guilty?" Sadalia called after the speeding car. "Huh? Isn't that how our system is supposed to work?"

Frustrated, she stuffed her notepad and pencil back into her bag. Althea came running over, and Officer Gore sighed. "Does *anyone* pay attention to the tape?"

"What tape?" Althea asked, and Officer Gore hung her head. She ushered the two girls back beyond the perimeter.

"What did you find out?" Althea asked.

"Nothing," Sadalia replied. "Except that Ian

and Barley were just taken away by the police."

"Arrested for grand theft school?" Althea said. When Sadalia looked at her with a questioning expression, Althea sighed. "You know, because they technically stole a school? By turning it into a dragon?"

Sadalia shook her head. "They didn't steal anything. And we don't know that they turned it into a dragon. We don't even know if they were arrested, for that matter!"

"What do you mean? The police took them away and everything! That looked like an arrest to me."

"That might be what it looked like. But I didn't hear anyone say, 'You're under arrest.' And before I got there, Officer Bronco and the elf woman were talking to each other. Ian and Barley were just standing by the police car. It was more like they were hanging out than in trouble."

"Poor, logical Sal," said Althea. "Why can't you just jump to conclusions like everyone else?"

"Look, Althea. I'm not saying that they're

innocent or that they're guilty," Sadalia began. "But if I want to be certainly certain, then I have to follow this story all the way to the end!"

"Which means . . ."

"It means interviewing everybody—anyone who saw anything! It means combing every square inch of town! It means leaving no stone unturned! No question left unasked or unanswered! It means finding out the truth, no matter where it takes me!"

Just then, Sadalia saw Principal Pipplemell walking past the yellow police tape, heading for her car. She seemed to be in a daze, shaking her head. Sadalia could hear her shouting, "My school! My job! My school! My job!"

Sadalia sprinted toward the principal, leaving Althea in the dust.

Chapter 4

"**P**rincipal Pipplemell!"

The school principal turned around and saw Sadalia running at her, notepad and pencil stretched out.

"Be careful!" the principal said. "If you trip, you'll poke your eye out! You're lucky you're not a cyclops."

Sadalia pretended she didn't hear her. "Excuse me, Mrs. Pipplemell, could I have a moment of your time? I'm writing an article for the school paper, and I—"

"No comment!" Principal Pipplemell said, holding up her hands.

"But you don't even know—"

"No comment!" Principal Pipplemell repeated. "If I say anything, it could be used against me! And there's already enough of that going on."

Sadalia was getting frustrated. What was with all the secrets? But she knew Principal Pipplemell. She was a big pushover if you knew the right things to say. Maybe she could get her to talk. "Okay. No questions about the events of today."

"Good," the principal said, wiping her brow and fiddling with the rollers in her hair. That was the first time Sadalia noticed Principal Pipplemell was wearing pajamas and a bathrobe, with fuzzy slippers. She had clearly driven to school in a hurry. She appeared relieved, her shoulders slumping.

"Let's talk about some of the students at New Mushroomton High," Sadalia said. "I'm certain you've heard of Ian Lightfoot?"

Principal Pipplemell glared at Sadalia. "No comment!"

"I'm not asking about what happened," Sadalia protested. "I just want to know what you think about him as a student."

Sadalia could tell that the words *No comment!* were once again about to be shouted at her.

Principal Pipplemell stood there for a second, then opened her mouth before closing it once more.

At last, the principal said, "He's . . . a student?"

"Are you confirming that he's a student, or are you asking if he's a student?"

"I know who he is! I'm the principal! I run this school with all the gumption a gnome can muster, so you can be darn certain that I know everyone here! For example, I know that his father passed away several years ago, and that his mother, Laurel, has raised him."

Sadalia was busy scribbling in her notebook when she saw Principal Pipplemell look at her. Then the woman started, like a wild animal. "Gargamon's Tail! I've said too much! How did you get me to talk? What are you, some kind of wizard?"

"No, ma'am," Sadalia said. "Just a reporter."

"Which is the exact same thing as a wizard, except you use words, not magic! And words *are* magic! So it really is the same thing!" Principal

Pipplemell said. "Now, that's all I have to say about Ian Lightfoot. If you'll excuse me, I have to grab some papers from my office. "

She stared at the pile of rubble and sighed before continuing. "Which are somewhere in there. What am I going to do? Kids can't go to school here. There *is* no school! Who's gonna pay for all this? I bet the school board tries to pin this whole thing on me. Well, I'm not going down alone!" Principal Pipplemell raged. "No, no, no! This gnome isn't just going to sit here and let things happen to her! I'll take everyone down with me!"

"Um . . . okay," Sadalia said, feeling uneasy. "I think I see some other people I should probably interview."

"I didn't do anything!" Principal Pipplemell said, completely ignoring Sadalia. "I was just sitting at home, watching a movie, minding my own business! It's not my fault the school turned into a dragon!"

"I didn't say it was," Sadalia said.

"That's just what you want me to think," Principal Pipplemell said.

"I'm going now."

"My school! My job! My school! My job!"

Sadalia turned around and ran, nearly crashing into someone as she turned a corner.

"Hey! You nearly plowed me over! I didn't survive the school turnin' into a dragon just so I could get flattened by the likes of you!"

Sadalia looked up and saw that she had run right into Mr. Gnash, a troll who worked as the night janitor.

"Sorry, Mr. Gnash. I didn't mean to run into you!" Sadalia said.

"No one ever does," Mr. Gnash said. "But they do. Oh, how they do."

Sadalia realized he could be a good source. "Since I've got you here . . . I'm working on a story for the school paper. What can you tell me about what happened tonight?"

"What can I tell you?" Mr. Gnash said, his eyes practically bulging out of their sockets. "We just witnessed the event of all time, that's what I can tell you! It's the return! The return of *magic*, Sadalia Brushthorn!"

"You . . . you know my name?" Sadalia said, taken aback.

"Of course I know your name," Mr. Gnash said. "I know everyone's names. I'm the janitor! I also know that you crumpled a piece of paper and tossed it into a garbage can, but you missed it, and I had to pick it up off the floor. Not that I keep track of stuff like that."

"Uh . . . no, of course not," Sadalia said. "Anyway. The return of magic! Do you really think that's what we just saw?"

"What else could it have been?" Mr. Gnash said. "I . . . I don't even know what to think! Should we run and hide? Jump for joy? Live in an underground bunker filled with a year's worth of food and water and maybe something to read until this all blows over? And will it *ever* blow over? If magic is back, is anyone safe?"

Sadalia was taking notes so fast she thought for sure the paper was going to catch fire.

"You seem scared," Sadalia said in a calm voice, trying to soothe Mr. Gnash's nerves.

But the janitor wasn't having it. "Of course I'm scared! In just a short time, the world as we know it has been stood on its head and slapped on the behind! Things will never be the same again."

Then he got in close and looked Sadalia right in the eye.

"I was inside the school when it started, Sadalia," he said quietly, his voice trembling. "I was inside. Do you have any idea what it's like to have your mop ripped from your hands, only to become the spine of some sinister magic dragon?"

"No," Sadalia said. "No, I don't."

"Well, you just be thankful, then. I'll never forget. And I don't know if I'll ever be able to set foot in that school again."

Sadalia looked over her shoulder at the massive pile of rubble that had been her school.

"I don't think that's going to be a problem."

Chapter 5

"So Principal Pipplemell wasn't much help, huh?" Althea said.

"None whatsoever," Sadalia replied. "She seemed to think the school board was gonna pin the whole thing on her. I think she's paranoid, maybe?"

"Seems likely." Althea nodded, unsurprised.

"Anyway, thanks for responding to my text, everyone. I know it was kinda last minute. But I need your help."

Althea, Parthenope, and Gurge made up Sadalia's main group of friends. They were all different—in personality, appearance, you name it—but they enjoyed hanging out together. Sadalia hoped that among them they could piece together the mystery that was Ian Lightfoot.

"Anything you need, Sal. What can we help you with?" Parthenope asked.

"Was he the kind of person to get in trouble?" Sadalia asked.

Kagar laughed. "Ian? Trouble? Those are two words that don't go together at all. If anyone was gonna get in trouble, it was his older brother."

"Barley?" Sadalia asked. "How so?"

"You know, he's always getting busted for stuff. Like, he's always getting in the way of the construction crews, trying to prevent them from tearing down historical landmarks and stuff."

"Do you know anyone who was close with Barley?" Sadalia asked.

"Yeah," Kagar said. "That guy."

"Who's 'that guy'?"

"That guy, standing right behind you."

Sadalia looked over her right shoulder and saw a towering figure behind her.

statement of fact. At least, she hoped that's what it was.

Kagar looked up at Sadalia. "Guilty as charged!" He laughed and stopped abruptly. "Sorry. I probably shouldn't make jokes like that. Not after what happened to Ian and his brother."

"How well do you know Ian?" Sadalia asked.

"Pretty good, I guess," Kagar said. "We're friends. We play Blazing Chariots all the time. He wanted me to come over to try out the new expansion pack for his birthday."

"Did you end up going to his birthday party?" She left out the part about how Ian had revoked her invitation.

"I couldn't go. My parents were taking me to the Labyrinth Mall. Big back-to-school sale, y'know?"

Sadalia nodded.

"That place is lame," Kagar added, walking around some rubble. "You can't find anything there. Which I guess makes sense, given the name and all."

troll named Kramm once. Big fella. Smelled like bananas."

"Did you see anything that happened at the school?" Sadalia asked, taking out her notebook.

"Me?" the centaur said. "Well, I was sitting here on this bench, minding my own business and blowing bubbles, as I do, when suddenly, I fell asleep. And when I woke up, all these folks were here."

Sadalia put her notebook away, sighed, and spotted Kagar standing about ten feet away.

"Great talking with you," Sadalia said, hurrying off. "Say hi to Kramm for me."

"Can't," the old centaur said. "Moved under a new bridge, left no forwarding address."

"Hey, Kagar!" Sadalia shouted at the satyr. "Do you have a second?"

"Sure," he replied. "What's up?"

"So, rumor has it you're friends with Ian Lightfoot." It wasn't a question. It was more of a

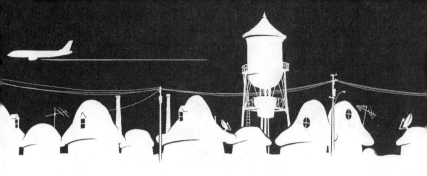

murmurs and rumblings from the assembled citizens.

"—heard it was all because of that Lightfoot kid—"

"—that was the craziest thing I ever saw! Never thought I'd see real magic up close—"

"—I always knew that Manticore was up to something—"

"—kid climbed that fountain just the other day, made a spectacle of himself—"

"—I can't look at my pet dragon the same way again!"

She saw one old centaur sitting on a bench, blowing bubbles, which Sadalia thought was a pretty weird thing to be doing given all the chaos.

"You look like someone who's looking for someone else," the old centaur said, pointing the bubble wand at Sadalia.

"Uh, yeah," she said. "I'm looking for a kid named Kagar."

"A kid named Kagar, huh?" the centaur said. "Can't say I know anyone named Kagar. I knew a

Sadalia shook her head.

"There *is* this one kid," Gurge said. "What's his name . . . Kagar?"

"Kagar," Sadalia said, snapping her fingers. "I know him! At least, I think I do. I've seen him hanging around with Ian. Kagar . . ." Her voice trailed off, and she started to write on her notepad. "Is that spelled the way you think?"

"I don't know how it's spelled," Gurge continued. "But if anybody knows anything about Liam, I bet it's him."

"Ian," Sadalia corrected.

"You bet," Gurge said, giving a thumbs-up.

The drama of the evening sent the majority of New Mushroomton's residents to the town center as everyone tried to figure out what had happened. Sadalia didn't know how she would ever find Kagar among the hordes of onlookers, media, police, and construction crews. As she pushed her way through, Sadalia could hear

"How well do you know Ian Lightfoot? What's his character like?" Sadalia said.

"His character?" Parthenope echoed. "You mean like in one of those role-playing games?"

Sadalia was about to correct her when Parthenope started laughing. "I'm just having fun, I know what you meant! Honestly, I don't know much about Ian. He kind of kept to himself. We said hi and bye in the hallway sometimes."

Sadalia made the note on her pad, even if it wasn't especially helpful. "What about you, Gurge?"

Gurge shrugged. "I know he had a party that I didn't get to go to."

"I'm certain that someone knows something about Ian," Sadalia said, dotting her pencil on her notepad. "I just have to find them."

"What about Gooleg?" Parthenope asked.

"The bog beast?" Sadalia said.

"Uh-huh. Maybe he knows something about Ian. Or not. He's kind of more bog than he is beast, so I'm not sure how helpful he would be."

Chapter 5

"**S**o Principal Pipplemell wasn't much help, huh?" Althea said.

"None whatsoever," Sadalia replied. "She seemed to think the school board was gonna pin the whole thing on her. I think she's paranoid, maybe?"

"Seems likely." Althea nodded, unsurprised.

"Anyway, thanks for responding to my text, everyone. I know it was kinda last minute. But I need your help."

Althea, Parthenope, and Gurge made up Sadalia's main group of friends. They were all different—in personality, appearance, you name it—but they enjoyed hanging out together. Sadalia hoped that among them they could piece together the mystery that was Ian Lightfoot.

"Anything you need, Sal. What can we help you with?" Parthenope asked.

Chapter 6

"You know Barley?" Sadalia sputtered.

A giant troll stood behind her. While his size was intimidating, he was smiling at her. He chuckled. "I do, indeed. The name's Shrub Rosehammer. I heard you were looking for me."

"How'd you find out?" Sadalia said, puzzled. "I didn't even know I was looking for you until just a second ago."

"Yeah, me neither," Shrub replied. "I was just walking by and I overheard your conversation with Kagar."

Sadalia immediately launched into reporter mode. "So, did you witness what happened here today?"

"Yeah, I did. I had gone out for a walk, trying to brainstorm some new campaigns. I got near the school, and . . . wow. I can't even . . . It was possibly the most amazing thing I've ever seen! Barley must have one crazy story to tell."

"What can you tell me about Barley Lightfoot? Is he mixed up in this situation?"

"I don't know if I'd call it a 'situation,'" Shrub said, surveying the ruins of the school. "More like a scene from the Battle of Stonemeade."

Sadalia scribbled down *Battle of Stonemeade?* on her notepad. "Getting back to Barley . . ."

Shrub nodded. "Yeah, well, I've known Barley forever. Since we were kids. You know *Quests of Yore?*"

Sadalia wrote the name on her notepad. "Of course. Everyone knows about *Quests of Yore.* It was a really popular board game a few years back."

Shrub immediately raised his eyebrows, somehow standing taller than he already appeared. "*Was* really popular? Try *is* really popular! You want to know why?"

What Sadalia really wanted was to get information about Barley. But if the only way she could get it was by listening to Shrub Rosehammer talk about *Quests of Yore*, then that's what she was going to do. She was a reporter, after all, and would do anything to get her story.

"That's because *Quests of Yore* isn't just a board game. It's a historically based role-playing scenario! It has formed an entire community of adventurers all over the realm, which makes it very important."

"I get it," Sadalia said, making a note of it.

"You can learn a lot from playing *Quests of Yore*," Shrub continued. "Like, all about magic, for instance."

"Magic," Sadalia said, intrigued. "Is that what you think was going on here today? Magic?"

Shrub tilted his head. "You know, it's just possible that's *exactly* what happened. How else do you explain the school suddenly transforming into a fire-breathing dragon?"

"Mass hypnosis? Or hysteria?" Sadalia offered. She didn't believe either one was responsible, but she was a reporter—it was her job to ask questions and poke holes in theories until she discovered the truth.

Shrub shook his head vigorously. "No way. First off, if it was mass hypnosis, wouldn't everyone be squawking like griffins?"

Sadalia wrinkled her nose. "I don't think that's how hypnosis works."

"Anyway," Shrub said dismissively, "what we saw was no illusion, no hoax, no imaginary story. It was full-on, straight-up magic. And with magic comes . . . curses."

"But how can you be so sure?" Sadalia asked. "Where's your proof? And wait—what? Curses?"

"Look, you don't play *Quests of Yore* for ten-plus years without learning a little something about magic. That's the only thing that can explain it."

"But magic and curses aren't—"

"Aren't what? Real? Of course they were real— *are* real. Back in the day, everyone used magic all the time, for everything."

"If it's so important, why did it become obsolete?"

"Because it was hard to learn! You couldn't just flip a switch to get light. You had to have the magic gift *and* learn how to do the spell. It took real skill and patience to become a mage."

"So, instead of casting the Light Spell, we have the light bulb," Sadalia said.

Shrub nodded. "You got it. Things just aren't like what they used to be. Did you know dragons could breathe fire more than a hundred feet? And the heat was so powerful that it could melt through solid steel? Now dragons are all domesticated and small, and you're lucky if they can even give off a spark. Don't get me wrong. They're adorable, and I'm definitely a dragon person, but this is what happens when everything becomes convenient and easy. No one wants to take the time to go on valiant quests or learn magic."

Shrub stopped to take a breath. "But that's how I know that what we just witnessed was total magic, through and through. That high school dragon completely fit the description of a real dragon of the days of yore. Except without the weird, goofy face."

"And what do you mean by curses?" Sadalia asked.

"Well, if you're not careful, it's real easy to unleash a curse when you're working with magic," Shrub said. "It's the price you pay when dealing with things that are powerful and rare. Only a curse could've created a beast like that one."

Sadalia made note of curses, then tapped her pencil thoughtfully.

"How do you think Barley got wrapped up in this?" Sadalia asked, trying to get her interview back on track.

Shrub thought about it for a few seconds. "Knowing Barley, it must have something to do with his kid brother. He loves that little guy. He'd do anything for him."

Sadalia smiled. Though she only knew Ian a little, it made her feel better to hear such a glowing testimonial, especially since the brothers were now on their way to jail. Maybe the story would reveal just how good Ian and Barley really were and convince the police to let them go!

"Let's back up a little," Sadalia said. "Let's say that what happened here today was a part of one of your *Quests of Yore* . . ." Her voice trailed off as she searched for the right word.

"Campaigns?" Shrub offered.

"Right, campaigns. Let's say this was one of your campaigns. This would be the end, wouldn't it?"

"Yeah, that sounds about right," Shrub said. "This would be the end of the campaign, where the dragon is defeated and the fellowship gathers the spoils of victory. Or, you know, gets arrested by the cops."

"Then what was their actual quest like?" Sadalia wondered. "How did it all start?"

Shrub's eyes lit up. "Like all good quests, it must have started at the Manticore's Tavern!"

Sadalia had heard some of her friends talking about the Manticore's Tavern a while back, but she had never been there herself. She wondered why it was so important.

Shrub continued, "You don't just wake up one day and say, 'I'm going on an adventure, and look! I just happen to have a map and all the details and an adventuring party ready to go.' No, you have to find out about it first. And the Manticore's Tavern is usually where that happens. A group of adventurers walks into the tavern and maps out a quest."

"So . . ." Sadalia said, leading Shrub.

"I'll bet you five unicorn crystals that Barley went to the Manticore's Tavern," Shrub said. "Now it makes sense why the Manticore herself showed up at the battle. I'm so jealous! I'd give anything to stand in my armor next to the legend herself. But it was enough of a gift to see her in action with my own eyes. And she even wielded the Curse Crusher! I never thought I'd see the day."

Sadalia was excited about this new lead. "Are you certain about this?"

"Yeah, of course!" Shrub said. "It all makes sense! Barley would *have* to go there at the start of the quest, otherwise there'd be no quest! Plus,

I heard there was a fire there yesterday. That's always an indication of something adventurous!"

Sadalia was surprised. "Fire? How bad was it?"

"I'm not sure, but I heard it was pretty serious. The whole place is off-limits."

Sadalia made note of the Manticore's Tavern. Just because it had suffered a fire didn't mean she wasn't going to check it out.

She was just about to wrap up her interview with Shrub when a thought occurred to her. "How did you find out about the fire?"

"From my sister," Shrub said. "Her best friend's cousin has a friend whose sister was a bridesmaid at this bachelorette party they had there last night. Well, there was *supposed* to be a party, anyway. But then the fire happened, and they had to call it quits. Didn't even get to do any karaoke, which apparently was a major bummer."

"Shrub, I'd really like to talk to your . . ." Sadalia said, checking her notes, "sister's best friend's cousin's friend's sister, and her friends, too. Any idea where they are right now?"

"Uh, let's see," Shrub said. "My sister says that group likes to hang out at Burger Shire. They come for the burgers but stay for the fun, friendly atmosphere."

"Thanks, Shrub!" Sadalia said. "I really appreciate it. Oh, and could I get your contact information in case I have any other questions?"

Shrub hesitated. "Well, it's not really the kind of thing I give out, but . . . I guess if it's for a quest, I can't argue with that." He wrote his phone number in Sadalia's notebook.

"Any chance you might have Barley's number?" Sadalia said. "To get this story right, I'm going to need to talk to him."

Shrub looked at Sadalia, nodding. "I sense the goodness in you, Sadalia. And I *would* give you his number. Except Barley's phone has gone off on the great adventure beyond."

"Great adventure beyond . . . ?"

"Fell in the toilet."

Sadalia thanked Shrub and watched as the hulking troll ambled off. She saw Kagar milling about nearby and went over to thank him for the tip about Shrub.

"Interesting guy," Sadalia said.

"The most interesting," Kagar agreed.

"You wouldn't happen to have Ian's phone number, would you?" Sadalia said. "Looks like I won't be able to call Barley."

"Yeah, the toilet, I heard," Kagar said. "I have Ian's number in my phone. . . ."

Kagar pulled up Ian's information and showed the screen of his phone to Sadalia. She dialed the number on the spot, but it went straight to voicemail. She'd known it would be a long shot.

Sadalia thanked Kagar and raced off toward her scooter, which was parked in the distance.

Chapter 7

Burger Shire was a local hangout, and there were always plenty of people around, even in the late-night hours. Sadalia couldn't wait to get there and question the bachelorette party. She just hoped they'd be there.

Unfortunately, she was going to have to wait because her scooter broke down. It seemed like her scooter was *always* breaking down. It wasn't new or even secondhand. The scooter had belonged to her mother, who then passed it down to Sadalia's older sister, and then it had sat in a storage unit gathering dust and cobwebs for years. Finally, one day, Sadalia's mom presented it to her with a broad smile on her face.

"It's been in the family for ages," she said. "And now it's yours!"

Sadalia was grateful; after all, she was happy

to have the ride, and a way to get to school and around town without having to constantly ask her parents or her friends. Still, the contraption had seen better days. But one good thing about having transportation that broke down at least once a day was that Sadalia had learned how to fix it, and fast. She pulled over to the side of the road, made some adjustments, and got the scooter back up and running.

Soon enough, but not soon enough for her liking, Sadalia was at Burger Shire. She parked the scooter and entered the restaurant. There were a couple of customers in line ordering food, and one cranky-looking gnome sitting at a corner table, just staring at the burger in front of him. It seemed far too big for him to fit into his mouth. He was contemplating exactly how he was going to eat it. He'd pick it up, try to get his mouth around it, fail, then set it back down and sigh.

Scanning the room, Sadalia saw them. A table of young women, just picking at their food. They looked like they were barely awake, as if they hadn't slept in a couple of days.

That's gotta be them, Sadalia thought.

She ran right over to the table of dazed women. "Excuse me," Sadalia said quietly. "I don't mean to intrude, but I'm looking for a bachelorette party that visited the Manticore's Tavern last night."

An elf met Sadalia's eyes. "We were at the Manticore's Tavern."

"Who are you?" asked a satyr.

"My name is Sadalia Brushthorn, and I'm a reporter for *The Fortnightly Dragon*," she said. "I was talking with Shrub Rosehammer, and he said that his sister's best friend's . . . his sister knows someone who attended the bachelorette party."

"Shrub Rosehammer's sister?" said a goblin. "Rose Rosehammer? You're friends with her?"

"I just spoke with her brother a little while ago," Sadalia continued, sidestepping the question. "He said that you and your friends were at the Manticore's Tavern yesterday and witnessed the fire?"

"Witnessed?" the goblin said, incredulous. "WITNESSED? More like NEARLY DIED!"

The table of women murmured in agreement.

"What can you tell me about the fire? Do you remember any details?"

"I remember the karaoke machine was busted," said a cyclops. "That, and the kracken kracklins were cold. I hate cold kracklins. But you know what I hate more?"

Sadalia shook her head.

"Buildings that are on fire! Specifically, buildings that I AM INSIDE that are on fire! I just wanted a fun bachelorette party with my friends, but instead, we got trapped in an INFERNO!" the cyclops bride-to-be wailed as she burst into tears.

"How did the fire start?" Sadalia asked. "Do you remember?"

The goblin put an arm around her friend, trying to comfort her. "Our friend here is getting married in a week."

"Congratulations," Sadalia offered. The bride nodded, wiping her tearstained face.

"So we thought, why not head over to the Manticore's Tavern for a fun night of karaoke? Then the Manticore—she's the owner of the place—went completely nuts and ripped off the head of the Manticore mascot, and torched it."

"Torched it?" Sadalia asked. "Deliberately?"

"I don't think there's another way to torch something, so, yeah," said the goblin. "Anyway, she torches the head, and throws it onto a table. Then she set a banner on fire. *Whoosh.* The rafters go up in flames."

"And what did you do?" Sadalia asked, writing it all down.

"What did we do?" the goblin said. "We ran for our lives! We grabbed each other and headed for the nearest exit, along with everyone else."

"I'm never going back to that place," the bride said, shaking her head.

"From the sound of it, no one will," Sadalia said.

"What do you mean?" the goblin asked.

"Well, the tavern burned down, didn't it?"

"Not as far as I know. After we ran outside, the fire department showed up pretty fast. They were able to contain it. It looked like they lost only the front of the building. You could see the original stonework peeking through."

"So it's still standing?" Sadalia asked, clarifying.

"Still," the goblin confirmed. "You can go check it out for yourself, if you want."

"Thanks, I will!" Sadalia exclaimed. "Did you see what prompted the Manticore to torch the mascot's head?"

"No," the bride said, raising her head from the table. "It was all a blur. But you might ask the sign twirler."

"The who?" Sadalia said.

"The sign twirler," the bride repeated. "Y'know, the person who stands outside Burger Shire twirling the sign around that says they have the best griffin burgers in town?"

"What would the sign twirler—"

"He was the one inside the mascot suit last night at the Manticore's Tavern," the goblin said.

"I guess he's out of a job, so now he's twirling signs here at Burger Shire. Anyway, if anyone knows what was going on and what set off the Manticore, it's probably him."

"Where is he now?" Sadalia said, noticing there was no sign twirler outside at this hour.

Everyone at the table shrugged. Sadalia thanked the group and then walked over toward the counter.

"Welcome to Burger Shire," said a cheerful elf behind the register. "Would you like to try one of our delicious shakes?"

"No, thanks," Sadalia said. She was impressed and a little confused as to why the employee was so enthusiastic at this hour. "I was just wondering when the sign twirler would be working again."

"I knew it!" said the elf. "Sign twirlers really do attract customers! He'll be here tomorrow at 6:30 a.m., sharp. Why don't you come by then and have a breakfast combo?"

"I just might!" Sadalia said, feeling optimistic. Then she headed out the door.

As she walked toward her scooter, her mind was racing. It had been a productive outing, even if she was going to have to make another trip out to Burger Shire in the morning to interview the sign twirler.

"Looks like Shrub knows what he's talking about," she said to herself, adjusting the chin strap on her helmet.

Then she felt her phone vibrating in her pocket. She was prepared to ignore it—it was getting late, and she was exhausted. She wanted nothing more than to fall into bed and get a good night's sleep before hitting the road the next morning to find the Manticore. But something about the call seemed odd to her. It was just a hunch, but as a reporter, she'd learned to trust her hunches.

She took out the phone and saw a missed call from Mrs. Nightdale. Sadalia called her right back. "Hi, Mrs. Nightdale? Sorry I missed your call. What's up?"

"Sadalia! I'm glad I reached you! Or that you

reached me. You know what I mean. Anyway, tell me you're working on a story!"

"As a matter of fact, I am," Sadalia replied. "And it's a pretty big one! Maybe the biggest ever!"

"That's great," Mrs. Nightdale said. "What a relief! How soon can you turn it in?"

"I'm kind of just getting started. It's about Ian and Barley Lightfoot, and the school turning into a dragon, and—"

"That's perfect! Perfect! It's just what we need for our front-page story! We go to press in two days, so you'll need to file it first thing that morning."

"In two days!" Sadalia exclaimed, panicking. "But . . . but I'm just starting! Why does it need to go to press so soon? We don't even have a school now!"

"Oh, that doesn't matter. If anything, it's now even *more* important that we operate as normal. The students and parents will be looking to us for information in this strange time."

"But it will take at least a week to—"

"You have two days," Mrs. Nightdale said. "You know, our next editor in chief should probably have a story like this under her wings before she takes over the paper."

Then she hung up.

"Editor in chief . . ." Sadalia said softly to herself. She smiled.

That would make her the youngest editor in chief *The Fortnightly Dragon* had ever had. And that position could open a lot of doors for her. The last editor in chief had received a journalism scholarship to Willowdale College!

This was what Sadalia had been waiting for: confirmation that this story would truly be her big break. It was her chance to prove that she was more than just a school reporter; she was a *true* journalist who could make it out there in the real world. She would have never guessed that a magical high school dragon would be the source of that break, but she'd always known she had to ready for anything.

Sadalia could hardly contain her excitement,

which was only slightly muted when she tried to start her scooter and absolutely nothing happened.

"Are you kidding me?" Sadalia said as she got off the scooter and started making adjustments.

After about ten minutes, it became clear that the scooter wasn't going to cooperate. At all. So she called her mom and asked for a ride home.

Chapter 8

Sadalia started her day before sunrise the next morning. She had stayed up for two more hours going over her notes and then spent another hour in bed, just lying there, thinking about everything. She didn't fall asleep until the early hours of the morning, and then woke to her alarm blaring at 6 a.m.

Her mom had given her use of the minivan that day, for which Sadalia was thankful. The minivan wasn't exactly a prized possession, but her mom had extracted a promise that Sadalia would return the van without a scratch on it.

She hopped in the driver's seat and drove over to Burger Shire. The store was just opening at 6:30 a.m. when Sadalia arrived. She pulled into a parking spot and saw the sign twirler emerge from the front doors of the restaurant. Sadalia got out of the car and slammed the door.

"Excuse me! Sir!"

The elf dressed as a griffin burger turned around to see Sadalia running right at him, clutching her notepad and pencil. He was holding a big sign that read, BEST GRIFFIN BURGERS IN TOWN! TWO FOR THE PRICE OF ONE! He suddenly dropped the sign and fell to the ground, crouching with his hands over his head. "What do you want?"

"Hey, don't freak out," Sadalia said. "I'm just here to ask a few questions. I'm a reporter."

"A reporter?" the burger asked, looking up at Sadalia.

"Yeah, a reporter. I didn't mean to scare you. I'm really sorry about that."

The burger slowly lowered his arms from his head, then reached over to pick up his sign. "It's all right. I'm just a little, uh, on edge after what happened the other day."

"Yeah, about that," Sadalia said. "I spoke to a group yesterday, and they said they were at the

Manticore's Tavern for a bachelorette party two days ago."

"Totally true," said the burger. "The karaoke machine wasn't working, though. They were really upset about it."

"So the Manticore ripped the mascot costume? And set it on fire?"

The burger looked at Sadalia and nodded. "I knew once that happened we weren't gonna fix the karaoke machine. I mean, how could we? There was a melted Manticore head, and the whole place was gonna go up in flames. Those women—they were so disappointed. I don't blame 'em."

"Can we talk about something other than the karaoke machine for a minute?" Sadalia asked, getting frustrated.

"Like what?"

"Like, for example, what's your name?"

"Oh, that. It's Darmot."

Sadalia nodded. "So getting back to the fire . . ."

"Yeah, about that. I was really bummed

73

because the karaoke machine really gets people excited to be there. And I have a whole routine I do, like a dance kind of thing. And everyone loves it. LOVES. IT. They all line up for photo ops with me, and kids want to give me high fives. And happy people means tips, which makes *me* happy. It's basic math, you know?"

Sadalia sighed. This interview wasn't going the way she thought it would. In fact, she wasn't sure it was an interview at all. But she realized she couldn't just quit. A good reporter knows how to make the most out of any situation, no matter how bad or hopeless it might seem.

"Was there anyone else there that night that you can remember?" Sadalia asked. "Anything out of the ordinary?"

Darmot thought for a moment. "Well, my boss, the Manticore? She was having this conversation with these two elves, and I think that's what upset her and made her rip off my head and set fire to it. I mean, not my real head. If that happened, I wouldn't be here talking to you now, dressed like a griffin burger, would I?"

"Probably not," Sadalia said. "So, those two guys . . . any idea who they were?"

"Egan, I think? One of them was named Egan. And the other one, a big guy, he was . . . Barmey."

"Egan and Barmey?" Sadalia said, writing it down. "Do you think it could have been Ian and Barley?"

Darmot shrugged. "I mean, maybe? It's pretty hard to see or hear anything inside that Manticore suit except for the karaoke. And the applause. I miss the applause. Do you think anyone applauds when you're dressed as a burger and spinning a sign?"

"No, I guess they wouldn't," Sadalia said.

"And another thing about this sign," Darmot said, pointing at it. "It's so heavy and bulky! How can I do any kind of artistic spins or flips when I can barely even hold it? When I said something to my new boss, he told me to keep my opinions to myself or I'd be looking for a new job. Anyway, so now I'm here. At least I'm making money. But no karaoke, no routine, no applause."

"Is there anything else you remember? Anything out of the ordinary?" Sadalia said, desperate to get any additional information.

"Well, the small one, Egan? I think he used . . ." Darmot paused dramatically. He leaned in close to Sadalia's ear, then whispered, "Magic!"

"Magic?" Sadalia repeated at full volume.

"Not so loud!" Darmot said, trying to shush her. "Then everyone will know!"

"So?" Sadalia said. "It's not like magic's against the law."

"Yeah, well, with my luck . . ." he said, his voice trailing off.

"What makes you think he used magic?" Sadalia asked.

"He said these words, and I remember them exactly, because I wasn't wearing my mascot head, so I could hear everything. He said, '*Aloft Elevar!*' "

"*Aloft Elevar?*" Sadalia repeated, writing it down. "And how do you know that's magic?"

"One, I play *Quests of Yore*, and that's one of the spells," he said. "I gotta research my part, right? And two, when Egan said it, a blast of light came out of the staff he was holding, and it froze a burning beam right in midair."

Sadalia recalled the staff Ian was wielding during the dragon battle. He was performing magic even before that event then. She wondered how long this had been going on.

"Anything else?" Sadalia asked, ready to put her notepad away.

"OH!" Darmot shouted. "There was a pair of pants!"

"A pair of pants?" Sadalia repeated. "Could you be more . . . specific?"

"No," the elf said. "It was just a pair of pants, walking around all by themselves! They had a top half at first, but then Barmey ripped it off. I was so shocked that I crashed into a waiter."

"Are you sure?"

"Of course not. Like I said, once you have that mascot suit on, you can't really be sure of

anything you see or hear. Like, one time, I thought
I saw a phoenix eat one of the customers."

"What was it?"

"Well, it wasn't so much a phoenix as it was a
feathery hat that a kid was wearing."

"Thanks for your time," Sadalia said, anxious
to pursue the story.

"No problem. It's one thing I have plenty of.
Now that I don't have the karaoke or applause."
Then Darmot held the sign up and started to
twirl.

Chapter 9

Sadalia hopped back into her mom's minivan and turned the key. The vehicle started without a problem, which actually surprised her. She was so used to her scooter breaking down every five seconds that something working correctly seemed out of the ordinary.

She zoomed onto the expressway, enjoying the freedom of the traffic-free lanes. This early in the morning, it would be easy for the minivan to speed toward the Manticore's Tavern and get there way before traffic began to pile up. And with her deadline in place, speed—and time—was of the essence.

She was going over a mental checklist of interviews she'd already done and interviews she needed in order to complete her piece on Ian and

Barley. Suddenly, her thoughts were interrupted by a loud *POP!*

If Sadalia had been remotely sleepy from getting up so early, she wasn't anymore. The minivan suddenly swerved to one side, and she had to fight the wheel as she hit the brakes, pulling over to the side of the road.

Looking carefully to make sure no cars were approaching, Sadalia opened her door and went outside to take a look. One of her rear tires was flat.

"I can't believe it," Sadalia groaned. She kicked the tire in anger and frustration. It helped nothing, of course. It only hurt her toe.

"Ow!" she cried.

A second later, Sadalia heard the *whoop whoop* of a siren. She turned her head, and sure enough, pulling up right behind her was a police cruiser.

Great, Sadalia thought, *just what I need—a ticket, on top of everything else.*

The police car door opened, and a tall cyclops officer stepped out. Then the passenger door opened, and there was a shorter satyr officer. This one she recognized.

It was Officer Gore from the school!

"Hey, Officer Gore," Sadalia said. "What brings you out here?"

"Sadalia," Officer Gore said, tipping her hat. "We were just cruising by and saw a motorist with a flat tire. Thought we might be of assistance. Imagine my surprise to find out that it's you!"

"It's a small world," Sadalia said.

"And how do you two know each other?" the other officer asked.

Officer Gore told her partner about how Sadalia had ignored the police tape at the school and almost gotten her in hot water with Officer Bronco.

"Well, I'm Officer Specter," the other cop said. "And I don't tolerate any funny business, so don't even try it. Just putting it out there."

"Noted," Sadalia replied. "Well, I'm sure you two must have better things to do than talk to an intrepid school reporter on the side of the expressway." She was hoping they would leave so she could change her flat tire and be on her way.

"Actually, no," Officer Gore said. "At the moment, we are one hundred percent not busy. So if you need a hand, well, we've got four!"

Sadalia looked at them both and smiled. "Well, I've got a jack in my trunk and a spare tire. Could you, I don't know, watch the road to make sure I don't get sideswiped by a semitruck?"

Officer Gore tipped her hat. "Happy to." She walked back to the police cruiser and popped the trunk. Then she pulled out a few orange safety cones and placed them behind Sadalia's minivan while Officer Specter kept her eye on the traffic.

Sadalia loosened all the bolts on the tire before placing the jack under the minivan. As she pumped it, the left rear tire slowly raised off the ground.

"Where you heading in such a hurry?" Officer Gore asked, hands in her pockets.

"I'm working on a story right now," Sadalia said as she removed the rear tire, rolling it off

to the side. "Got a tight deadline, so I gotta make every second count."

"Sounds important," Officer Gore said, interested. "Can you give me a hint what it's about?"

"Well, it kind of involves you, to be honest," Sadalia said. She wasn't sure if she should even be admitting the subject of her story, given the resistance she had encountered earlier.

Officer Gore brightened. "What, like an 'Officer of the Year' kind of thing? Me? Really? That's . . . that's an honor!"

"It sure would be," Sadalia said, "but that's not exactly what I'm writing." She stood up, walked to the trunk, and took out the spare tire. It bounced when it hit the ground, and Sadalia rolled it over to the left rear of the minivan.

Officer Gore deflated a little. "Oh, sure, well, that would have been kind of sudden, anyway."

Sadalia placed the tire on the axle. "I'm actually writing about what happened at school. The thing with the dragon."

"Alleged dragon," Officer Specter grunted from several feet away.

"Specifically, I'm working on a story about Ian and Barley Lightfoot," Sadalia said, hoping it would provoke a reaction from Officer Gore.

"Those two? They're in a heap of trouble," Officer Gore said. "Especially that Barley. But I probably shouldn't say anything else."

"Can you give me one of those bolts?" Sadalia asked. Officer Gore handed a bolt to her, and she took it in her grease-covered fingers. "And of course, I wouldn't want you to say anything that would get you into trouble. I just thought maybe you might be able to fill me in on what kind of boys they are. Background stuff."

"Background stuff?" Officer Gore said. "Well . . . I guess, as long as we don't talk about the, you know . . ."

"ALLEGED DRAGON," Officer Specter shouted.

"Right, that," Officer Gore continued, an annoyed look on her face. "As long as we don't talk about that, I think it would be okay."

"Great!" said Sadalia as she put the wheel back on and tightened the bolt. "So, you said that you know Barley?" Then she put out her hand, asking for another bolt.

"No," Officer Gore said, shaking her head. "I mean, we don't really *know* him, but we know him by reputation. He's always getting into some kind of trouble, protesting this, complaining about that. Like that whole fountain business."

"What 'whole fountain business'?" Sadalia asked.

"Sorry, that falls in the category of *stuff I shouldn't say anything about.*"

Sadalia nodded her head. "So what can you tell me about Ian, then?"

"Well, we ran into him a couple nights ago."

"Where was this? At the school?"

"This was out on the expressway," Officer Gore said. "He was driving a purple van. Studying to get his driver's license, apparently. Officer Bronco was with him."

"That's Officer *Colt* Bronco?" Sadalia clarified. She motioned for another bolt, then tightened it.

"That's the one," said Officer Gore. "Said that he was taking Ian out for some 'driver's education drills,' I think he called them. But the kid was swerving all over the road."

Sadalia was confused. Why would Officer Bronco be teaching a random teenager how to drive? Was he a police officer by day and a driver's ed instructor by night? She asked Officer Gore to elaborate.

"Oh, Bronco is dating Laurel Lightfoot, Ian and Barley's mom," Officer Gore said. "Seems like he's having a rough time, by the sound of it."

"Yeah, I gave him some advice about that," Officer Specter added. "It's not easy being a stepparent. But the whole interaction was suspicious."

"What do you mean?" Sadalia asked, standing up. She grabbed an oily rag from the back of the trunk and wiped her greasy hands clean. Then she put it down and pulled a small notebook and pencil from her back pocket.

"Bronco was a little out of it. Ian was even more out of it. He was wearing all these big, puffy clothes, and he was just wandering around."

"And you say Barley wasn't there?"

"No, no sign of him. It was just Officer Bronco and Ian," Officer Specter said. "And that's not even the weirdest part!"

Sadalia could tell both officers were warming up. She furiously jotted down notes and hoped that they'd keep talking.

"Well, last night, when we saw Officer Bronco? On the ground. There were hoof prints."

"That's not unusual," Sadalia said, puzzled. "I mean, he's a centaur. He has hooves."

"Right," Officer Specter said. "But when we looked at the trail of prints, it suddenly changed to sneaker prints."

"Sneaker prints? You mean, like he suddenly put on sneakers over his hooves?"

"Exactly. Which makes no sense. You seen that guy's feet? No way he could wear sneakers. Not ones that would match those footprints we saw, anyway. I got suspicious, so I radioed in to Bronco."

"And?"

"And he said that he was never on the expressway. And that he was never with Ian or with us."

"That doesn't make any sense," Sadalia said, hastily scribbling down some notes. "Maybe he just didn't remember?"

Officer Specter shook her head.

"She's right," Officer Gore said. "Colt? I mean, Officer Bronco? Forget something like that? Not likely. Guy's got a steel-trap mind. Even if he is juggling a new family and all."

"You've been a huge help, Officer Gore," Sadalia said. "You too, Officer Specter."

"Any time," said Officer Gore. "Looks like your tire's all fixed up!"

Sadalia opened the door to the minivan and hopped inside. Before she could turn the key, Officer Gore said, "I think you're in trouble, miss."

Sadalia's heart leaped into her throat. What was she talking about? She hadn't done anything wrong! "What is it?"

"You left that jack under your car," Officer Gore said. "Won't get very far like that."

Sadalia laughed, then hopped back out of the van and worked the lever so the jack would come loose. She put it in the trunk of the car and closed it.

"Thanks for the catch," Sadalia said, and the officers waved at her. She got back into the minivan and gave a thumbs-up to the officers. "Thanks again for everything!"

As she was about to drive off, Sadalia had a thought. "Wait, I saw Officer Bronco with Ian and Barley after the incident. And I'm guessing that Laurel Lightfoot was the other one with them. Couldn't Officer Bronco help get the boys out of trouble? With him being in a position of authority and all?"

"He'll probably do his best for Laurel's sake," Officer Specter said. "But this is bigger than him. I hear that the mayor is asking for someone to be held responsible. Those boys caused some serious damage."

While Sadalia pondered this latest information, the radios on the officers' uniforms blared, *"Calling Officers Gore and Specter, Gore and Specter."*

Officer Gore answered the radio. "This is Officer Gore, copy."

"There's been a robbery at a pawn shop," said the operator. *"Proprietor's name is Grecklin. Said someone took a sword worth a considerable amount of money. It's called a 'Curse Crusher.' We need you to go and take her statement."*

Curse Crusher? Why does that name sound familiar? Sadalia thought. She began flipping through her notes. She knew she had heard that name before. *Yes! Shrub mentioned that the Manticore was wielding the Curse Crusher during the battle. But why was it at a pawn shop, and how did it end up with the Manticore? Who stole it?* If this was connected to the high school incident, Sadalia needed to check it out before the police could interfere.

"Copy that," Officer Gore said. "But that's a pretty far drive for us. Aren't there any units closer?"

"*Define 'closer,'*" came the response over the radio.

"Like, someone who isn't as far away as we are?" Officer Gore said.

There was a brief pause, and then the operator said, "*You want to get coffee first, don't you?*"

Officer Gore shifted her feet uncomfortably. "Uh, any word on the Lightfoot boys?"

"*They're being taken downtown for processing.*"

Downtown? thought Sadalia. *That can't be good!*

"I've gotta fly, officers! Good luck!" Sadalia called out as she put the minivan into drive and took off down the expressway.

Chapter 10

The clock was ticking. The deadline was looming. The minivan was . . . running with no further flat tires.

Sadalia knew she had to get to the Manticore's Tavern, but she needed to follow up on this new lead immediately, while it was still hot.

She gunned the engine, giving the minivan as much gas as she dared. Crossing her fingers, even her toes, Sadalia hoped she'd make it to the pawn shop before the police did. It helped that the officers were probably going to stop for coffee along the way—that would give Sadalia a chance to beat them there.

But when she looked up the shop using the owner's name on her phone, she saw that it really *was* a far drive. It would take her at least a couple of hours. She would need a lot of luck if she was going to stay ahead of Officers Gore and Specter.

Thankfully, her mom's minivan kept chugging away, and soon enough, Sadalia had pulled into the parking lot. The shop was rundown and dirty—the windows were so cloudy and covered with faded advertisements that she couldn't even see anything inside. Sadalia wondered how the shop got any business.

She parked the minivan, hopped out, and ran to the front door of the pawn shop. She heard a bell ring.

"Don't touch anything!" came a voice from the back of the shop.

Sadalia froze. "Even the floor?" She couldn't help herself.

"Of course you can touch the floor," said a grizzled old goblin, emerging from behind a shelf filled with teacups. Grecklin was the owner of the shop. She had a scowl on her face and was moving exceptionally slowly. "How else are you gonna walk around here and find something to buy so I have money for dinner?"

"I'm not here to buy anything," Sadalia started. "I—"

"Then you're not here," Grecklin said, and turned around.

"My name's Sadalia. I'm with my school's newspaper. And I wanted to ask you some questions about your recent robbery."

Grecklin looked at Sadalia and furrowed her brow. "You heard about that? News travels fast. I only called the cops about it a couple hours ago."

Sadalia couldn't help smiling a little. "Yes, well, I'm really interested to know what happened. I'm wondering if it might be connected to the incident at the school."

Grecklin moved closer to Sadalia, looking her in the eye. Sadalia noticed the pawn shop owner kept both arms down at her sides, somewhat stiffly, and was barely lifting her feet off the floor when she walked, if at all.

"Are you . . . all right?" Sadalia asked.

The goblin rolled her eyes. "I'm fine. Mind your

own business." She shuffled toward the counter. "Blasted Manticore venom."

"Manticore venom?" Sadalia asked, interested.

"Yeah, Manticore venom. You ever been stung by the Manticore?"

Sadalia shook her head. "I didn't even know about the Manticore until yesterday."

"Well, I have," Grecklin said. "Can't do anything with my hands, and I can barely feel my feet. She said it would only last an hour! But of course, you can't trust a thieving scoundrel like that."

Instantly, Sadalia's mind started racing. The Manticore had been here, but why would she stop at this random pawn shop after her tavern had just burned down?

"Can you tell me what happened, exactly?" Sadalia said, whipping out her notepad and pencil. She started to write, but then the tip of her pencil snapped. "Uh . . . you don't happen to have a pencil sharpener I could use, do you?"

Grecklin moved to rub her chin with her right hand. But the hand was still numb from the

Manticore venom, so all she really did was swat herself in the face. She winced and put her hand back down. "Yeah, there's one behind the cash register you can use."

"Thanks," Sadalia said, walking toward the register.

"For two shards," Grecklin added, smirking.

"You're charging me two shards to sharpen my own pencil?" Sadalia asked in disbelief.

"It might be *your* pencil, but it's *my* pencil sharpener," Grecklin said. "That's the offer, take it or leave it."

Sadalia sighed. She dug into her pocket and found some loose coins. She threw them on the counter by the cash register and counted them out. "There. Two shards exactly."

"Just leave it there," Grecklin said. "Sharpen your pencil. Hurry up. I don't have all day."

One sharpened pencil later, Sadalia was standing next to Grecklin, feverishly taking notes. "So there

I was, minding my own business," said Grecklin, "when this elf woman walks in. Now, I've never seen her before. And then the Manticore comes in with her. They seemed to be in a real hurry."

"In a hurry . . . why?"

"How should I know? They were looking for something called the Curse Crusher."

"What's a Curse Crusher?" Sadalia asked.

"Well," Grecklin said, "I'm gonna go out on a limb and guess that it's something that crushes curses."

Sadalia wasn't in the mood for sarcasm, but she realized the only way she could get information from Grecklin was to play along. "This Curse Crusher. What did it look like? Can you describe it?"

Grecklin nodded. "It's a sword. I don't know, about so high," she said, stretching her arms as wide as she could. "Nothing fancy to look at, but the Manticore really wanted it. I told them they could have it for ten."

Sadalia tilted her head slightly. "Ten? That seems like a reasonable price."

"Ten thousand, I mean."

"Ten thousand!" Sadalia cried, trying to imagine anything in this shop full of dusty old microwave ovens, clock radios, and rusty armor being worth ten thousand *anything*. "Isn't that a little . . . high?"

"Look, I don't set the prices, I just sell the stuff," Grecklin said.

Sadalia stared at her.

"Okay, obviously I set the prices, too," Grecklin offered. "But I gotta make a living! Rent's not cheap!"

"So what happened when you told them the sword would cost ten thousand?"

"The woman said something about needing the sword for her sons."

Sons, Sadalia thought. It was looking more and more likely that this woman was Laurel Lightfoot, Ian and Barley's mother. She flew in with the Manticore during the battle and then was talking to Officer Bronco before the boys were taken away. But Sadalia wondered how the Manticore and Laurel even knew each other. They seemed like an odd pairing.

"So did they pay it?" asked Sadalia.

"If they paid it," Grecklin said, "do you think I would have called the cops? Not only did they steal from me, but that monster stings me on top of it!"

"Wait a minute," Sadalia said, checking her notes. "When I first asked how much the sword cost, you said ten. Not ten thousand."

Grecklin shrugged. "I must have forgotten. Maybe the Manticore venom got to my brain and made me all goofy."

"I don't think that's what happened at all," Sadalia said. "I think you offered ten, and when you found out they needed the sword, you jacked up the price."

Grecklin appeared indignant, flopping a hand against her chest. "Do I look like the kinda person who would cheat somebody?"

"Yes."

"Touché."

"Did they pay *anything* for the sword?" Sadalia asked.

"Yeah, they left, I don't know . . . ten?" Grecklin said.

"So it's not like the sword was stolen. More like you didn't get to rip off a customer like you'd hoped."

Grecklin rolled her eyes. "The Manticore said it was the only sword of its kind and was forged of some rare metal. Only a fool wouldn't have raised the price after hearing that. And Grecklin is no fool."

Sadalia was in the process of closing her notepad and putting it away when she heard the bell. The front door opened, and in walked Officers Gore and Specter.

"Hello?" said Officer Specter, looking around the shop. "We're here about the complaint of a stolen sword?"

Chapter 11

Before she could be spotted by the police officers, Sadalia managed to slip out the back door of the pawn shop. She ducked low, avoiding the windows, and went around to the front, where her minivan was waiting. She was surprised the police hadn't spotted it, then realized that a truck had pulled up in front of her van, blocking it from view.

She was avoiding the police, but she wasn't exactly sure why she was doing it. It wasn't like she had done anything wrong. Still, she didn't want to have to explain to Gore and Specter what she was doing at the pawn shop, and how she had gotten there before they had.

She opened the door to the minivan and started it up, hoping the noise wouldn't draw the attention of the officers. The pawn shop door didn't open, so Sadalia figured she was safe. She drove off, letting out a sigh of relief.

Based on what she'd learned from Grecklin, the Manticore and Laurel were definitely working together. Why did the Manticore need the Curse Crusher, though? Had she known about the dragon in advance? If so, was there a chance this was the Manticore's fault and the boys were just in the wrong place at the wrong time? Either way, there had to be a connection somewhere.

With each interview, Sadalia felt like she was getting more pieces of the puzzle. But she had no idea how those pieces fit together or what image they made. And time was running out. It was already noon. If Sadalia was going to file her story in the morning, she was going to have to get to the Manticore's Tavern—and fast.

The minivan seemed to be on her side, as it only gave her one hiccup: the gas light turned on just a mile away from the tavern. She made a mental note to return the van to her mom with a full tank. She didn't want to give her mom any reason to get upset about the van. But she didn't have time to worry about that now.

She pulled up to the Manticore's Tavern and was surprised by how much of the building still remained. Sure, you could tell there had been a fire, but the place looked like it could be rebuilt. It was cordoned off by yellow police tape. The facade of the building had burned away, and the front of the tavern was still smoldering. The ground was wet, indicative of the water the firefighters had used to put out the flames. The place looked completely deserted. Which, of course, made sense. Why would anyone come to a closed, fire-damaged tavern?

Sadalia's heart sank. She had placed a lot of hope on the Manticore's Tavern, thinking maybe it would reveal some secret that would help her unlock and solve this mystery. But it looked like it was going to be a big bust.

She opened the door of the minivan and shut it behind her, then walked through some puddles on the ground, toward the front of the tavern.

Then she heard it. A rustling sound. Like someone was looking for something, digging, shifting debris.

Lifting the yellow tape, Sadalia ducked under. She looked around. The sound was coming from inside the front door.

She went inside. It was dark, so she used the flashlight on her phone to light the way.

"AHHHHH! FALDAR'S HORN!"

Sadalia jumped at the sound of the roar and fell backward, hitting the ground. She dropped the phone, and the flashlight turned off.

"What are you doing here?" said a booming voice.

"What am *I* doing here?" Sadalia asked. "What are *you* doing here?"

"I own the place!" the voice said, and through the darkness, Sadalia saw the Manticore standing before her.

"You're . . . the Manticore!" Sadalia exclaimed, stating the obvious. She was much larger than Sadalia had realized, but she could see where the Manticore had softened over the years.

She wasn't quite the hulking, muscular warrior that was depicted in the soot-stained portrait on the wall. But Sadalia now understood why Shrub Rosehammer had been in such awe of the Manticore. The relics that survived the fire displayed her legendary battles and conquests. And after what she had witnessed the day before, Sadalia definitely wouldn't want to cross paths with the Manticore in battle.

"It wouldn't be the Manticore's Tavern without the Manticore," the beast said. "And you are . . ."

"Sadalia. I'm a reporter for *The Fortnightly Dragon*."

The Manticore looked down at Sadalia, then extended her hand. Sadalia took it and stood up. "Thanks. I didn't mean to scare you."

"Same here," the Manticore said. "So you're a reporter, huh? What are you here to report on?"

"I'm doing a story on the big battle that took place at the high school yesterday. Specifically, the two boys, Ian and Barley Lightfoot. They've been taken into police custody, and—"

"Police custody?" the Manticore said. "Sadalia, I think you might have that a little wr—"

"I know what I saw," Sadalia protested. "Now, I figure if I can piece together what happened, and tell their story, I might be able to help them. Will you help me do that?"

"I don't know," the Manticore said, turning her attention to the smoke-damaged restaurant. "I've got a lot of work to do if I'm going to reopen the business any time soon. Maybe come back tomorrow."

"Tomorrow will be too late!" Sadalia exclaimed. "I have to turn in my story by morning! And who knows what will have happened to Ian and Barley by then?"

The Manticore sighed with a heave of her shoulders and stared at Sadalia. "I bet you won't leave until you get your story, will you?"

"A good reporter wouldn't. And I'm gonna be one of the best. Maybe even editor in chief."

"All right, then," the Manticore said, and Sadalia thought she could see the faintest trace of a smile. "Fire away. What do you want to know?"

Sadalia dug into her pocket, pulling out her notepad and pencil. "How did you meet Ian and Barley?"

"Simple. The two of them came to my tavern looking for a map."

"A map? A map to what?"

"A map that would show them the location of a Phoenix Gem."

"What's a Phoenix Gem?" Sadalia asked.

"Reporters ask a lot of questions, huh?" the Manticore said. "A Phoenix Gem is what wizards call an assist element. It's something that's used in spellcasting. Powerful spellcasting."

"*Spellcasting* spellcasting? Like, as in magic?" Sadalia asked.

"Like magic," the Manticore said. "In fact, I hadn't seen magic like that in centuries. It really took me back." She smiled as she reminisced about the old days.

Sadalia was confused. "Centuries! How old are you?"

The Manticore chuckled. "A lady never reveals her age. The ol' wings may not work as well as they used to, but I think I did pretty well in that battle. Maybe I'll sign up for a gym membership. Nothing like good old-fashioned combat training to get back into shape."

"Sorry, I didn't mean to be rude," said Sadalia. "I guess I don't know much about you. But there were some people I've run into who seem to idolize you. Why is that?"

"Well, not to toot my own horn, but I was one of the most famous warriors in history. My tavern was a place where warriors, rogues, and wizards alike would gather to risk life and limb for the mere taste of excitement! I was dangerous and wild—no one could tame me. Actually, I have young Ian Lightfoot to thank for reminding me of that."

"What do you mean?" asked Sadalia.

"I didn't want to give the boys a map at first. I had a lot of responsibilities, and I wasn't about to risk my tavern for anything! But Ian pointed out that risk and adventure used to be my whole life. I realized I didn't even recognize myself anymore. I was Corey, not the Manticore. And so I may have overreacted just a little and burned my tavern on my road to self-discovery. All of a sudden, I couldn't stand seeing all these reminders of how I had sold out. I guess I had to light a literal fire under myself to get things going again!"

"So what happened after the fire? Did you give the map to Ian and Barley?"

"Well, the *real* map, the one they wanted, was destroyed in the fire. But I told them that my children's menu is based on the real thing."

"Children's menu?" Sadalia said.

The Manticore walked to a charred wooden counter and reached over it. She pulled out a stack of papers, peeled one off the top, and handed it to Sadalia. It was wet, stained black around the edges from soot and ash.

Sadalia was scribbling as fast as she could. "So why did Ian and Barley need the map, and what did they want with a Phoenix Gem?"

The Manticore didn't say anything for a second. She stayed quiet and looked at the paper menu in Sadalia's hands. "I think that's really for the boys to say. You'll need to ask them directly. But let's just say that it's something deeply personal, and perhaps the best reason ever to undertake such a dangerous quest."

"A dangerous quest?" Sadalia asked. "Is that what they were on? A quest? Like that game, *Quests of Yore?*"

"It's no game," the Manticore said. "No, it's far more real than that. Tooth of Zadar! Is that the time? I need to go!" The Manticore headed to the door. "Look, you'll just have to ask them yourself, okay? Anyone who takes the Path of Peril instead of the easy way deserves my respect. It's a true judge of character. Only those with strong hearts could have survived that and vanquished a dragon, all in the same day."

"Path of Peril?" Sadalia asked. For the first time since she'd started working on the story, Sadalia wasn't sure if it was something she should

really pursue. A place called the Path of Peril didn't seem like something to trifle with. A voice in her head was screaming at her, saying, *LEAVE THE STORY ALONE, SAL!*

She knew what it was.

It was fear.

Swallowing hard, Sadalia swore she wouldn't back down. She'd come this far. She had to follow the story all the way to the end, no matter what.

She dashed after the Manticore and was about to ask another question. Suddenly, the Manticore raised her hands, as if to stop Sadalia. "Sorry, I don't quest and tell. I gotta get going. This tavern won't get up and running again on its own." She unfurled her massive wings, ready to take off.

"Wait!" Sadalia called out. "Please, one more question!"

The Manticore turned around and looked at her. "One more. But only because I sense you have a good heart. And you kinda remind me of myself."

Sadalia smiled. "Your, uh, accomplice at the

pawn shop. The woman at the school, the one who was riding on your back with the Curse Crusher sword. Who was that?"

"I think you already know," the Manticore said. "But just so it's official, that was Ian and Barley's mom, Laurel."

With that, the Manticore turned and took off into the sky.

Chapter 12

Sadalia sat in the minivan, trying to decide her next step. Should she risk going to the Path of Peril? If she didn't go, what would her next lead be? And even if she decided to go to the Path of Peril, her "map" wasn't exactly helpful. All it featured was a few activities for kids to figure out while they wait for their meal. How was this based on the Manticore's real map?

Maybe I can ask someone how to get to the Path of Peril, Sadalia thought. *It can't be that hard to find, right?* If Ian and Barley really used the same menu to find a Phoenix Gem, then maybe she could follow it to find out more about the weird events that had occurred.

The decision was obvious.

"Looks like I'm off to the Path of Peril," she said aloud, instantly realizing that it sounded

115

dangerous and maybe wasn't such a great idea. But she was going to do it anyway.

She glanced at the children's menu. She worked out one of the activities, which gave her the answer RAVEN'S POINT. Sadalia knew Raven's Point was a mountain off one of the major expressways. She realized Ian and Barley must have taken the Path of Peril to Raven's Point. But why would the boys take some ancient and terrifying-sounding road instead of taking the paved—and non-perilous—expressway? It had to have been something quest-related—some kind of knowledge that she didn't have. She would need to figure out how to get to that path.

But first, she needed to sort out the gas light situation. She searched for and then stopped at the nearest gas station, called Swamp Gas.

She pulled up to the pump and got out of the minivan, then removed the cap from the gas tank. While she waited for it to fill up, she took out the notepad from her pocket and removed the children's menu, unfolding it. Sadalia looked at Raven's Point.

She knew a little about ravens. Of course she knew that they were birds, but she also knew they were considered something of an ill omen. That didn't make her feel especially great. But she was willing to do what she needed to get the story.

The gas done pumping, Sadalia folded the menu and stuck it back inside her notepad. She looked over at the gas station store.

That's when she saw them: sprites.

They were no bigger than water bottles, but they were scarier and tougher than beings even four times their size. Wearing leather jackets, they looked to be part of a motorcycle club. Squinting, Sadalia saw the words PIXIE DUSTERS emblazoned on the jackets.

As she walked into the store to buy some snacks, she couldn't help overhearing the sprites' conversation. They were talking about motorcycles, but one of them said something strange. "Just think. If we hadn't met those two, we'd still be driving everywhere forever."

It wasn't much. Just a simple sentence, tossed

out quickly. But it stuck in Sadalia's mind, and she was sure that it had something to do with Ian and Barley.

She went over to the counter. A clerk stood behind it. He looked up at Sadalia and sighed. "Don't mess anything up. I just spent an hour cleaning up the joint."

"I wasn't going to," Sadalia said. "I mean . . . I just wanted to buy something."

"Well, what are you buying?" the clerk asked impatiently.

Sadalia was still watching the sprites. One of them had taken an interest in her minivan and was walking around it now.

"Um, I'll take some Sparkle Sticks." She reached down into a cardboard box on a shelf under the checkout and put a bunch of the brightly colored candies on the counter.

"Just like those Pixie Dusters," the clerk said, mumbling. "Don't even have motorcycles no more. They just come in here for the Sparkle Sticks. That'll be three even."

Sadalia paid, grabbed the candy, and ran outside. She approached the sprite inspecting her minivan.

"What are *you* staring at?" the sprite demanded.

"I could ask you the same question," said Sadalia, sounding braver than she felt. "That's my minivan. Well, it's my mom's minivan. I usually ride a scooter, but it sort of died on me yesterday. I'm gonna save up and get a new one, though. Maybe even a motorcycle one day, like you guys."

"You ride, too, huh? Sweet," the sprite said, kicking the left rear tire. The tire wobbled.

"Yeah, I wouldn't do that." Sadalia winced. "That's a spare. Basically held on with invisible tape and wishes."

The sprite smirked. "Ha! That's pretty funny, Scoots. My name is Dewdrop."

"My name is Sadalia. I'm a reporter for *The Fortnightly Dragon.*"

"Nah, I like Scoots better."

"Okay . . ." said Sadalia, not trying to push the issue. "I'm actually out here following a story. I was wondering—can I ask you and your friends a few questions?"

Dewdrop's eyes narrowed. "I don't trust reporters. But you *are* a fellow rider and all. . . ."

"I brought these," Sadalia said, showing Dewdrop the Sparkle Sticks.

That sold it. Dewdrop took the Sparkle Sticks from Sadalia's hand. "We're all yours, Scoots. What do you wanna know?"

"I heard one of your friends over there say something about you learning how to . . . fly, is that right?"

Dewdrop's eyes darted over to the other sprites standing by the door. She shot one of them a look that said, *I told you to stop flapping your big mouth.*

"Dewdrop?"

"Yeah, yeah. Well, see, it's like this. We were here at the gas station yesterday, when a few guys stopped by. One big elf, one small elf, and another weirdo wearing sunglasses who had major attitude. And Shades? He knocked over our bikes. Now, as a fellow rider, I don't have to tell you that

NO ONE TOUCHES OUR BIKES. NO ONE! If I ever get my hands on that guy . . ."

Sadalia tried to be sympathetic. "Yikes, no! Who would do that?"

"Shades! Shades did that!" Dewdrop replied. "Anyway, the situation was not looking good for those three, as far as living was concerned, when Tiny Elf said we were lazy and started insulting our ancestors. Stuff like that. I could've taken him, but the big elf picked up Tiny and carried him away."

Sadalia paused. "Wait, what? One of the elves *carried* the other one away? And why are you calling him tiny? No offense to you or anything, but elves are my size."

Dewdrop looked her up and down. "Yeah, the big one was around your size. But Tiny was my height. Don't ask me why he was so small."

Sadalia didn't know how to respond. It didn't make any sense. "We might come back to that. But it sounds like things got pretty heated. What happened after your bikes got knocked over?"

"We chased after the three of them on our motorcycles."

"They were driving a car?" Sadalia asked.

"Van," one of the other sprites chimed in.

"What did it look like?" Sadalia asked. "Color? Did it have any identifying marks?"

"It was purple," Dewdrop said. "And there was a pegasus painted on the side."

That matches the van I saw when Barley picked up Ian from school, Sadalia thought, *and it matches Officer Gore's description.*

"Anyway, we chased 'em down the highway for a few miles, but they managed to escape. That was pretty annoying. I hate when people do that," Dewdrop said, her lip curling into a sneer. "Still, if it hadn't been for them, we never would have known that we could still fly."

"If you can fly, what are you doing at a gas station?"

"Got a lot of questions, don't you, Scoots? We need flying snacks, of course. Now that we're exercising these babies, we need more energy."

Dewdrop fluttered her wings for emphasis.

Sadalia smiled, taking notes, then stopped. Something was bothering her. "So there were three people last night?"

"Yeah, three," Dewdrop said. "The big one, the small one, and Shades."

"What can you tell me about Shades? Was he young? Old? Was he an elf, too?"

"That wise guy," Dewdrop grumbled. "He must be their leader. He was all covered up. I couldn't really see him. Lucky for him. But he was shaking his fist at us as we were trying to catch 'em. What a jerk. How about you guys?"

Dewdrop looked at the other sprites, and they all murmured in agreement.

"Huh," Sadalia said, genuinely perplexed. This story just kept getting stranger and stranger.

"Look, the Pixie Dusters have gotta fly. 'Cause we can now," Dewdrop said. "Keep exploring those open roads, Scoots."

Sadalia smiled at the sprite and watched as she and the rest of the club took to the skies.

Whoever this third person was, it definitely added a new wrinkle to the story. Sadalia decided to pop back into the gas station to see if she could find out anything else from the clerk.

"I don't know anything," the clerk said, sounding bored.

"Anything?" Sadalia pressed.

"Anything," the clerk confirmed. "It's a minor miracle I'm able to work here."

"Okay," Sadalia said, writing on her notepad. "Then can you at least tell me whether or not there were three customers here last night at the same time as the Pixie Dusters?"

At the mere mention of the sprites, the clerk said, "I don't know anything!" repeating his previous statement, but in a considerably more panicked tone.

"It's okay. The Pixie Dusters already told me some of the story. You don't need to worry about them."

The clerk just stared at her.

"Anyway, anything else you can tell me?"

"I do recall that there were a few customers here when the Pixie Dusters were, uh, spreading their charm last night. But I couldn't tell you what they looked like. They were pretty well-mannered, though."

"Do you have a security camera or anything?" Sadalia asked.

"What, you mean, like, check the footage to see if these customers who you think were here were actually the customers who were actually here?" the clerk asked.

It took a second for Sadalia to understand exactly what the clerk was trying to say. "Yes?" she said, still not quite sure.

"Well, yeah, we do have the security footage," the clerk said. "But I'm not supposed to show anyone. My manager would be really annoyed if I did that."

Sadalia's heart sank.

Then the clerk stepped out from behind the

counter and walked toward the back of the store. He motioned for Sadalia to follow.

"What are you . . ."

"I kinda feel like annoying my boss today."

"There!" Sadalia exclaimed. "That's them!"

They had fast-forwarded through about an hour of footage before she saw them. Ian and Barley, plain as day. Inside the gas station, buying snacks.

Well, Ian was buying snacks. Barley was just as tiny as Dewdrop had said. In the video, he jumped out of Ian's shirt pocket and carried a key over his head to the bathroom. And in the bottom corner of the frame was someone dressed in a hooded sweatshirt—wearing sunglasses.

So this confirms that there were three of them, Sadalia thought, *but who is Shades? And why wasn't he with them during the dragon battle?*

She thanked the clerk and raced out the door. But before she took off, she had an idea. She pulled out her phone and dialed a number. "Hey, Shrub? This is Sadalia, the reporter you spoke to yesterday. Have you ever heard of the Path of Peril?"

Shrub laughed. "Have I ever heard of the Path of Peril? What is this? Apprentice hour? It's *only* one of the most important roads in *Quests of Yore*. But it's pretty much abandoned now. Why are you asking?"

"I need to get there. Could you tell me how?"

"Ooh, now we're talking!" exclaimed Shrub.

Sadalia smiled. She knew she could count on Shrub's knowledge and enthusiasm. He gave her directions and wished her luck. Sadalia climbed inside the minivan and started the engine.

The Path of Peril was waiting.

Chapter 13

Sadalia knew that if she was going to head out on something called the Path of Peril, she had to expect a little peril to come her way. While she had yet to experience anything that quite approached peril, she was pretty sure her minivan was. Her mom's pride and joy was clearly not made for such a journey. While it might hum right along on a paved highway, it was another story entirely on this unpaved path. It was rocky, pitted, and just plain awful. The spare tire, which had already been a little wobbly, felt like it was close to falling off completely.

"Come on, come on," she said, offering words of encouragement.

The sun was already getting low, and Sadalia was getting worried. She still had to make her way to Raven's Point, figure out the identity of the mysterious third person, and put together what all of that had to do with Ian, Barley, and the dragon monster.

Ian and Barley.

What must they be going through? Sadalia wondered. Already being processed at the police station, locked in a jail cell, maybe even solitary confinement? Who knew?

And the story. The story that could help set them free. She was no closer to finishing it. In fact, she hadn't even started writing it yet. She'd managed to organize some of her notes the previous night before she went to bed, but that was about it. She was still certainly certain she could get it done in time, though. Even Mrs. Nightdale thought so.

But there was a little voice in the back of Sadalia's mind. It was whispering, *Give up. You can't do it. There's no way. Even if you write the story, what will that prove? It won't help Ian and Barley. You will fail, and not only will you not be editor in chief, but it will prove you're not a real journalist.*

Sadalia knew what the voice wanted her to do. It wanted her to quit.

But that was the last thing she was going to do. She had come too far. There was so much on the line. It wasn't just about the story, or even about Ian and Barley.

It was about proving something to herself. That she could do it. That she could be a real reporter. There was no going back.

As Sadalia drove along the Path of Peril, she did her best to keep the voice at bay, reminding herself of everything she had done so far. Of the people she had met, interviewed, and in some cases turned from angry, surly foes into potential friends.

She could do anything if she put her mind to it.

She saw the drawbridge first. Ancient. Worn.

Parking her mom's minivan, Sadalia opened the door and got out to stand on the rocky ground. She closed the door and walked ahead, getting closer to the bridge. She noticed that the ground ended.

"Please tell me that's not what I think it is," she said out loud, to no one in particular.

Sadalia slowly walked to the edge of the chasm. She picked a rock up off the ground. It was a geode, the kind that sparkled like it had diamonds in it. Sadalia tossed the rock up in the air a couple of times, catching it in her right hand. Then she threw it into the chasm. It was swallowed by the darkness. It became clear to her that if she was waiting to hear the rock hit the bottom of the pit, then she was going to be waiting for a long time.

"It's a bottomless pit," she said.

She could see Raven's Point in the distance. Using the drawbridge to cross this pit appeared to be the only way to reach her goal. She walked along the edge of the chasm, but not too close. Just the thought of accidentally stumbling and going over into the abyss made the hair on the back of her neck stand on end.

She thought about her mom and dad. The

sun was going down, it was getting dark, and she hadn't exactly told them what she was doing or where she was going. She'd only left a message on her mom's phone that said, *"I'm working on a school project. I'll be home late. Don't worry, I'll grab dinner here. Thanks!"*

Sadalia had never said where "here" was. And now, "here" was a bottomless pit along the Path of Peril.

Taking out her phone, she saw that there was no reception. The phone was essentially a brick. "Great," she said. Even if she had wanted to, there was no way to call her parents now.

The only way out was to go forward. But the old bridge had definitely seen better days. She didn't know if it could support her weight, let alone the van's weight. She wondered if she could jump the chasm with her minivan to get to the other side. It was a ridiculous notion, not least because the chasm was far too wide, and it wasn't like the minivan was made for death-defying stunts.

She walked over to the start of the drawbridge.

There she stood, gazing into the distance. Then she looked directly at her own feet, and then outward, to the first step on the bridge. She wasn't sure how sturdy it was.

"Only one way to find out," Sadalia said, and she was just about to put her foot on the bridge when she heard the voice. *Don't do it. Stay here. It's safe. You might fall! And even if you make it, you don't know what's on the other side!*

Sadalia balled her hands into fists, took a deep breath, and put one foot on the bridge. Then she told the voice to take a flying leap.

She walked a couple of steps onto the bridge, hearing the creaking boards beneath her feet. She didn't have much evidence that the bridge could support the van, but she had no other choice. Unless she drove across the drawbridge, there'd be no way to continue on the Path of Peril to find Raven's Point, a Phoenix Gem—any of it. She'd run out of time for sure, and she didn't want to be completely exposed in this deserted terrain without any kind of protection.

Taking a deep breath, she got back into the minivan, started the engine, and slowly rolled toward the drawbridge. She decided that she needed to stare straight ahead and keep focused on the other side.

"Just look forward, just look forward," Sadalia said to herself as she inched the minivan ahead. She heard the drawbridge creak beneath her vehicle, and she could have sworn that she felt the minivan sinking, like the bridge was giving way.

Taking a deep breath, she kept on giving the minivan gas, when suddenly, she heard a loud *SNAP!*

Chapter 14

Sadalia took her foot off the gas and hit the brakes. Then she rolled down the window and leaned her head out carefully. The wooden board beneath her left front tire had snapped. Sadalia wondered just how much stress this ridiculously old bridge could take. She could try to go back where she had come from, but that might cause the boards to collapse. The same thing could happen if she tried to drive on.

Either way, jeopardy was waiting. So what was it to be? Sadalia swallowed hard and hit the gas.

No other boards snapped on the way across the drawbridge. Miraculously, Sadalia made it to the other side without further incident.

When her mom's minivan was safely on solid ground, Sadalia turned off the engine and got out to look at the drawbridge. She fully expected it to collapse.

"I SO don't want to do that again," Sadalia said. Then she got back into the minivan and pulled out her notebook.

Her brain started to sort through everything she had discovered thus far, from all the people she'd spoken to in the past two days. But the one thing that stuck in her mind that she couldn't quite figure out—the thing that made absolutely no sense—was the weird sunglasses guy who was hanging around with Ian and Barley at the gas station.

She had no idea who he could have been. None of Ian's or Barley's friends or acquaintances had mentioned anyone who matched the description of Shades.

So who was it?

Then her brain started to make some connections that it hadn't before. When she had spoken to Officers Specter and Gore, they said they had encountered Officer Bronco and Ian on the highway. They hadn't mentioned anything about Barley. So where was Barley during all that? Hidden in the van, maybe? Elsewhere?

And then there was the matter of Ian. Specter had described Ian as being "out of it." No, those weren't her exact words. Sadalia looked down at her notepad, flipping through the pages. She came to the interview with the officers and checked her notes. She saw the scrawled words:

BRONCO = LITTLE OUT OF IT.
IAN = EVEN MORE OUT OF IT.
WEARING BIG, PUFFY CLOTHES—
WANDERING AROUND.

That meant Ian was all covered up, and the officers probably didn't get a very good look at him. Which meant there was a chance that maybe, just maybe, it wasn't Ian.

Then Sadalia thought back to the gas station and Shades. He was also covered up—she'd seen that much on the security footage.

Maybe Shades and "Ian" from the officers'

encounter were the same person! So if it wasn't Ian, and it wasn't Barley . . . then who was it?

Sadalia kept rolling that thought over and over in her mind until another one wormed its way in. Something else Officer Specter had said. She flipped through the notepad. Scribbled at the bottom of one page were the words:

HOOF PRINTS
SNEAKER PRINTS

That jogged her memory. Officer Specter had explained how the hoof prints on the ground had suddenly stopped and sneaker prints followed immediately after. Almost like someone's feet . . . *transformed*?

Sadalia shook her head. She was still getting used to the idea of magic, *real* magic. But she decided then and there that she would consider every possibility. After all, wasn't a reporter basically a detective?

"Hooves . . . sneakers," she said out loud as she put the notebook away.

Sadalia scratched her head, looking through the windshield at the jagged cliffs that surrounded her. She saw majestic mountains in the distance. It may have been called the Path of Peril, but Sadalia had to admit there was also something quite beautiful in her surroundings.

"What if the hooves *did* become sneakers?" Sadalia said, giving voice to her suspicion. "Because someone had transformed themselves to look like Officer Bronco. So who was it? Ian? Barley? Ian AND Barley? Holy Tooth of Zadar, what if it was BOTH of them disguised as Officer Bronco?"

That would explain why neither one of them was seen at the van. They were in disguise! And maybe Barley was tiny at the gas station because of magic, too! Sadalia didn't know why his size would help them at all, but magic *had* to be the reason for the strangeness of those situations.

But the mystery still remained: Who was Shades?

Picking up the notepad from the seat once more, she pulled out the menu and unfolded it.

She saw the circled words: RAVEN'S POINT. That was her destination. She could see the mountain peaks far in the distance. But there was no way her minivan could take her up those steep slopes. And it was even less likely that she could make it on foot with her deadline looming. How did Ian and Barley manage to get there so quickly?

For the first time since she had crossed the pit, Sadalia noticed something peculiar. Glancing at the top of the drawbridge, she saw what looked like a stone sculpture of a . . . what was that? A bird?

No, not just a bird.

A raven.

"What if . . . Raven's Point isn't a place?" Sadalia said. "What if it's the most obvious thing ever? Like, a raven pointing?"

Sadalia stared at the raven sculpture and noticed its beak extending outward. Then her eyes followed the direction in which the beak was pointing. She turned her head and looked off into the distance. Squinting, she could just make it out.

Another raven sculpture! Except it was facing another direction entirely.

Maybe the ravens would lead her all the way to . . . well, if Raven's Point wasn't a place, then where *would* it lead her?

Sadalia was so excited, so eager to pursue the puzzle, that she gunned the minivan in the direction of the second raven.

It all sounded so easy, and it probably was, except reality decided to intrude on Sadalia's adventure. In this case, reality was a set of tire tracks that she spotted on the Path of Peril.

And then the tracks *weren't* on the Path of Peril. Up ahead, she saw a wooden fence. Something had smashed right into it, and broken beams lay on the ground, the wood splintered. And there wasn't just one set of tire tracks. There were multiple sets.

Sadalia started piecing it together, figuring it must have been Ian, Barley, and Shades in their van, trying to follow the ravens, and someone following them.

Chasing them?

The police?

Sadalia stopped the van and got out. The tracks definitely veered off the path into the distance. Should she follow those tracks or continue following the ravens? As much as she wanted to follow the ravens, Sadalia knew that if she wanted to find out exactly what happened to Ian and Barley, then she needed to follow the tire tracks. If they went this direction, she should, too. Maybe they got back on track later on.

She drove slowly, making sure she stayed along the crisscrossing tracks. Clearly, several vehicles had driven this direction. She wondered what had led to this chase, and how they had even found Ian and Barley here.

Sadalia stopped when she caught a glimpse of the next raven. She noted the direction in which the raven's beak was pointing. Then she noticed that the tracks suddenly veered in that direction, toward a narrow mountain pass. *Ian and Barley must have seen the raven and realized*

they needed to get back on course, she thought. She turned toward the pass and drove on.

Sadalia began to feel nervous. It was nearly dark; the sun was setting, and once it was gone, it would be pitch-black on these treacherous mountain roads. If she couldn't put all the pieces of the puzzle together soon, her efforts would be for nothing.

The minivan was picking up speed when Sadalia rounded a corner. Suddenly, there was nothing in front of her. No path, no road, no tire tracks, no raven. There was only a massive mountain of boulders, as if the road itself had been swallowed whole.

Sadalia hit the brakes as soon as she saw the boulders, turning the steering wheel hard to the right. The minivan narrowly avoided the nearest boulder, and she shot forward in her seat, restrained by her seatbelt.

"No," Sadalia said. "No! NO!"

Chapter 15

"**I** can't believe this!" Sadalia shouted, kicking the boulder in front of her minivan.

How am I going to follow the tire tracks now? Or the ravens, for that matter? she thought. Time was wasting. It was dark already. And she couldn't even come close to driving her minivan over the boulders, which meant going on foot. That would slow her down even more.

Suddenly, it looked like going on Ian and Barley's quest was no longer an option. Her eyes filled with tears. For a moment, she had really thought she could do this. She had gotten the leads. She had found the Manticore. She had gone on the Path of Peril! But it was all for nothing.

Sadalia looked over at her notebook sitting on the passenger seat. It was filled with her detailed notes and theories and questions—so many questions that still remained unanswered. *Maybe I need to go at this from a different angle,* she thought. *Take a less obvious route. But I don't even know where to start.*

All she knew was that failure was not an option. She had sworn there was no way she was going to fail Ian and Barley, or herself. Not now. Not when she was so close to getting the story.

With fresh determination, Sadalia put the minivan in reverse and turned the vehicle around. It skidded in the dirt for a moment, sending the minivan over a large rock. The bump nearly sent Sadalia through the roof, and she felt like screaming.

Taking a deep breath, she headed back toward the drawbridge.

Unlike on her initial trip over the drawbridge, Sadalia decided to practically floor it across on the way back. She figured that if she went fast enough, she might avoid the problem she'd experienced on the way over.

Turned out she was right. The trip was dull and uneventful. But that didn't make Sadalia feel any better.

In fact, she felt terrible. She'd been through so much already, and to come so close only to have to pack it in . . . it made her angry.

After hours of maneuvering through the Path of Peril in the dark, Sadalia was finally speeding down the expressway. She was relieved to be back on paved roads.

As she drove, she started playing everything over in her head, sorting through the facts she had gathered so far. She still needed to talk to Ian and Barley and their mother. She figured that would be last—she could stop at the police station on the way home to write her story. But would she even be allowed to talk to them? She had been met with so much resistance before. Why would the police suddenly let her see them?

But what else was there? What was she missing?

Everyone said that the whole thing had started when the school turned into a dragon. But Sadalia realized that the whole thing had *really* started when Ian and Barley grabbed the map from the Manticore's Tavern. Possibly even before that.

So the boys had the map, and they'd found Raven's Point, or whatever the ravens were pointing at. Which was *what?*

Then she remembered: the Phoenix Gem. How had she forgotten? She had been so caught up in the quest, that's why. And not just Ian and Barley's quest.

No, it was Sadalia's own personal quest. The quest to become a journalist, a real reporter. She had become obsessed with all the little details, like the mystery of Shades. Sadalia had forgotten what the boys were after originally.

Assuming that they found the Phoenix Gem, where did they go next? She needed more information, but she didn't have it.

And judging by the flashing light on her

dashboard, she didn't have enough gas, either. She had done so much driving that day that the van was ready for a fill-up already. Meeting the sprites at the gas station felt like a lifetime ago.

Sadalia drove for another couple of miles, hoping that her mom's minivan wouldn't suddenly give up. Her luck held out, as she managed to make it to a gas station. Pulling up to the pump, she dug into her pocket. She only had a little money left, but it would be enough to buy a few gallons of gas and get her back home.

While she pumped the fuel, Sadalia noticed that there was a twenty-four-hour diner across the road. It was late, and she pulled out her cell phone. It looked like she finally had reception, but almost no power left.

That's when she noticed the missed calls and voicemails and text messages, all suddenly loading in now that she was back in range.

Her parents.

Sadalia groaned. "Where's a bottomless pit when you need one?"

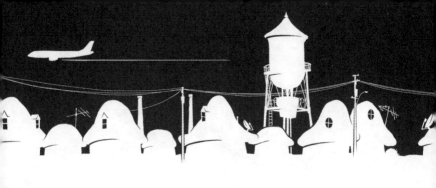

Her minivan gassed up, she drove across the street and parked at the diner. She closed the car door and took in a deep breath of night air. *What time is it?* she wondered, realizing she hadn't checked when she'd looked at her phone. She walked up the steps to the diner, reached for the glass door on the right, and gave it a yank. It wouldn't budge.

Then she heard someone call out from inside the diner, "The right one don't work!"

So she grabbed the handle of the left door and pulled. It opened, and she went inside.

Sadalia looked around and saw that it was almost entirely empty except for a cyclops sitting at the counter, drinking a cup of tea, and a satyr working behind the register.

"Don't usually get a lot of customers this time of night," the satyr said. "Have a seat at the counter. Want to order anything?"

Sadalia smiled. "I'm good, thanks. Actually, I

was hoping that I could maybe sit down for a few minutes and charge my phone?" She held up her cell phone and the dangling charge cord.

The satyr frowned. "I'd say you have to order somethin', but I don't see how that would come close to makin' a difference. Sure, go ahead."

"Thanks," Sadalia said. "This is about the only thing that's gone right tonight."

Sadalia walked past the counter, toward a booth. As she passed the only other customer, she saw that the cyclops was sound asleep, snoring lightly, his face just a few inches above his cup of tea.

"Don't worry about ol' Hendorrak," the satyr said. "He comes in here every night, orders a cup of tea, falls asleep. It's kind of his thing."

Sadalia nodded and sat down at the booth. She leaned down to plug in her charge cord and then put the other end in her phone.

Staring at the screen, Sadalia looked at the number of messages she'd received from her parents. Thirty-two calls. Seventeen texts.

She felt guilty. She didn't want to listen to the voicemails or read the texts.

"Time to face the music," she said, and she called her house.

Sadalia wasn't even sure if the phone actually rang. Before she knew it, her mother was on the other end of the line.

"Sadalia! Where are you? Do you have any idea how worried we've been? Do you know what time it is? It's after midnight!"

"Mom, I'm at the diner. I'm sorry—"

"Sorry isn't going to cut it! Come home now!"

"I didn't mean—"

"Are you all right? Are you hurt?"

"No, I'm fine, nothing bad happened—"

Sadalia could tell that her mother was relieved she was okay when her next question was, "What about my minivan? Any scratches?"

She thought about the flat tire . . . and the couple of small dents that resulted from the rocky terrain of the Path of Peril. Sadalia decided that those *technically* didn't count as scratches. "No, it's all good."

"Just come home, honey," her mother said. "Just . . . come home."

"I'll be there in a half hour," Sadalia said, then hung up the phone.

"That sounds fun," the satyr said. "Sorry, I couldn't help but hear you on account of the diner's complete lack of noise."

Sadalia nodded as her stomach gave a loud rumble. She realized she hadn't eaten all day. "I guess I'll take a burger to go," she said, defeated.

Chapter 16

There was one silver lining. At least Sadalia was returning the minivan in one piece. She couldn't believe it had held together as well as it did.

That was about the only good thing Sadalia could think of as she drove down the street toward her house. As she approached the driveway, she could see that her mom and dad were standing on the steps outside their front door, in their bathrobes, waiting for her. Their expressions showed a mixture of worry and anger, anxiety and who knew what else.

Sadalia felt awful. This was the first time in her life that she had ever done anything like this. She'd never even really been late before. But this was more than being late. This was a whole lot of things, all rolled into one.

She had left messages for her parents and told

them that she wasn't going to be home right away and not to worry about her. But she hadn't asked for permission before doing any of it. On top of that, she hadn't exactly been 100 percent truthful with them about everything she was doing, either.

She parked the minivan and trudged across the driveway, up a little stone path, and toward the front steps.

Steeling herself for what was to come, Sadalia decided that it was better to speak first. Maybe she could throw herself on her sword and her parents might show her some mercy. "Before you say anything," Sadalia started, "please know that I'm so sor—"

But she couldn't even get out another word before Sadalia's mom threw her arms around her daughter's shoulders. Her dad joined in, hugging the two of them. Their combined grip was so tight that Sadalia thought for sure she could feel something cracking, like maybe a rib.

"Don't. Ever. Do. That. Again," her mom said, punctuating every word.

"What she said," her dad added.

"I'm sorry, I'm so sorry," Sadalia said, and she was. "I got so caught up in getting the story, I totally lost track of time. Mrs. Nightdale told me that this was the kind of story that could set somebody up to be editor in chief of the newspaper, and I want that so badly, and I just . . . I made some bad choices, and you're always telling me to make good choices, and I did just the opposite."

"Shhhh," her mom said, patting Sadalia's back. "I know. There's a lot of pressure on you. And I know you want to be the best."

"Yeah," Sadalia said.

"We want you to be the best person you can possibly be, too," her dad added. "We want you to succeed. But we also want you to be safe. That's what parents do. It's our job to keep you around for as long as possible, y'know?"

Sadalia laughed. "I know, Dad."

"Now, look. It's late," her mom said. "It's time you got to bed. You need your sleep. We can talk about your punishment in the morning."

Sadalia's eyes opened wide. "Wait, what? Punishment? I thought you were just glad I was home safe!"

"We are glad, completely glad. And relieved. SO relieved!" her dad said, smiling.

"But you're still totally in trouble," her mom chimed in. "There's no getting around that, kiddo. At the very least, you're grounded. That means no leaving except for school and essentials."

Sadalia let out a big, heavy sigh that seemed to linger. "I guess I deserve that."

"Guess you do," her dad said, giving his daughter another hug.

Sadalia's mom had a slight smile on her face, and she gave her daughter a kiss on the forehead. "Go inside, honey. Sleep well. No staying up and writing, either."

Sadalia went up the stairs two at a time and headed for her bedroom. She ran inside, then closed the door. Wheeling the chair out from under her desk, she sat down. Then she reached around the back of her computer monitor and turned the system on. While it hummed to life, Sadalia set her notepad down on the desk and took out the children's menu from the Manticore's Tavern.

She booted up her word processing program and stared at the blank screen. She was ready to write. She stared at the blank screen some more. The cursor blinked on and off, just waiting for Sadalia to start typing.

"I have absolutely no idea what I'm going to write," she said. "Where do I even start with this?"

Her fingers grasped the notepad and she started to flip through the pages. She had covered an unbelievable amount of ground on her travels over the past couple of days, and she'd interviewed so many different people. There was Grecklin, the Manticore, the two police officers, Principal Pipplemell, the clerk at the gas station, Dewdrop. . . .

Sadalia's mind was racing. She had a ton of information, but there were still people she needed to interview. And they were the most important ones—Ian and Barley, for starters!

There was just no way she was going to be able to complete the story in the time she had, and get it right—*really* right—without getting those interviews and the answers to her questions. The story would be incomplete. And incomplete stories didn't help a person become editor in chief.

Pushing back from the desk, Sadalia stared at the blinking cursor on the blank screen. She took a deep breath, held it, then exhaled. *Maybe I'll check online to see if there's anything I can find out there*, she thought. If she was stuck in her room, unable to get out in the field to learn more, then maybe she could bring the world to her.

Opening the web browser, she did a search for *Dragon New Mushroomton.* Sadalia startled when she heard a light knock on her door. She quickly turned out the light and dove into bed just as her mom opened the door.

"You weren't working on your story, were you?" her mom asked.

Sadalia was quiet for a moment. "You know I was, Mom."

Her mom laughed softly. "Yeah, I know. Now I'm serious. You need your rest, and we need a break. Get to sleep, kid."

"I'm just gonna read for a little bit, then I'm gonna hit the hay," Sadalia promised.

Her mom gave her a look that said, *Okay, but just for a minute,* and then closed the door.

Leaping up from the bed, Sadalia scooted back into the chair by the desk and looked at the computer screen.

The screen was filled with news stories all covering the dragon battle in the town square. Sadalia clicked on the first story and skimmed through it. Then she went to the next story and the next. Each one contained more of the same information: *a dragon attack in New Mushroomton, the town is baffled, no one knows who is responsible, the Lightfoot family is somehow connected.*

As Sadalia clicked on the tenth link, she began to doze off.

Sadalia woke up with a start. Her clock read 3:27 a.m. She was annoyed with herself for wasting time, but it was clear that her brain and body had needed a break.

She moved her computer mouse, waking up the monitor. She felt just as stuck as she had a couple hours before. *Maybe I need to make my search more specific,* she thought. She typed *Barley Lightfoot* into the search bar.

She was surprised to see that the first result was a video. Sadalia quickly clicked on the link and the video window popped up.

The video was shaky, like an amateur had shot it. It looked as though it had been recorded on somebody's phone. But sure enough, there was Barley, clear as day, standing in front of the fountain in the middle of the town square.

Members of a construction crew were yelling at him, and so were a bunch of police officers who had gathered around the base of the fountain.

"I won't let you tear down this fountain!" Barley shouted.

"Get out of the way!" an annoyed construction worker hollered back.

"Ancient warriors on grand quests drank from its flowing waters!" Barley said.

Then the police officers yanked on Barley, grabbing at his legs and arms, and he fell into the dirty water.

Sadalia played the video again, watching it all the way through once more. Then she played it again. And again.

"The fountain," she said to herself. "Officer Gore mentioned this. . . ." Then she grabbed her notepad, flipping rapidly through the pages until she came across her notes from the interview.

BARLEY
ALWAYS IN TROUBLE/PROTESTING/
COMPLAINING
FOUNTAIN BUSINESS
"CATEGORY OF STUFF I SHOULDN'T SAY
ANYTHING ABOUT"
FOLLOW UP!!!!!

"I gotta check the fountain," Sadalia said. "There's something here."

She grabbed the children's menu, folded it, put it back in the notepad, and shoved it in her pocket. Sadalia was about to open her bedroom door when something suddenly dawned on her. *Oh yeah, I'm in massive trouble, and I'm grounded, and leaving the house right now is the world's WORST idea.*

So that was the end of it, then. If she listened to her parents, then she was done with the story. There'd be no checking out the fountain, no interviews with Ian and Barley or their mom, nothing. No editor in chief.

She had to get the story. There was no other option. Not when she was this close.

That's when she realized her mom had said that, yes, she was grounded. But she had *also* told Sadalia that she was allowed to leave the house for school and "essentials" only.

Was there anything more essential than breaking the story of the century?

Sadalia didn't think there was.

So she did what anyone in her position would do. She grabbed a bunch of pillows and pulled up the covers over them to make it look like she was sleeping in the bed. Then she opened her bedroom window, climbed out onto the roof, and scampered down to the ground.

Chapter 17

Sadalia wished her scooter was working so she wouldn't have to walk. At least she could have quietly pushed the scooter down the block, away from the house, and then started it up. But that wasn't an option.

And the minivan was out of the question. There was no way she could take that—not without her parents' permission, which she could never get because she wasn't supposed to leave the house. That left her own two legs.

So she walked down the street in the early morning hours, heading for the fountain. She realized she had never walked around her neighborhood at this time. Everything was so peaceful and serene. If she hadn't known better, she never would have guessed that a dragon had attacked the town only two days before.

As Sadalia approached the town square, she had no idea what she was looking for. Maybe something about the fountain—the history of it—would trigger some further investigation.

Having grown up in New Mushroomton, Sadalia knew she'd been through the town square countless times, but she'd never really paid attention to the fountain aside from tossing coins into it to make wishes. She looked at the town square now and saw debris everywhere from the dragon battle. There was construction equipment all around, but it was otherwise deserted.

Sadalia stood up on the edge of the fountain in order to get a closer look. The fountain was topped with a spire, and there was something at the top of the spire—a sculpture that looked kind of like an eyelid. It was open.

She climbed up to the top so she could peer inside the chamber. The space wasn't very big, but it looked as though it had once held something. There was dust around the edges, except for in the middle, where an object must have been resting.

"Hey," came a bored-sounding voice from below.

It completely startled Sadalia, who had been lost in thought. She nearly lost her balance, but grabbed on to the spire.

"Oh, hello," she said, looking down at an elf construction worker. She was wearing a hard hat and looked at Sadalia with suspicion. "Lovely morning."

"I s'pose," the construction worker said. There were three other construction workers walking over, and they all sat down around the edge of the fountain.

"You're probably wondering what I'm doing up here," Sadalia said nervously.

"No," the construction worker replied. "We're on break."

But Sadalia pressed on. "I'm a reporter for *The Fortnightly Dragon*. I'm doing a story, and I wanted to ask you a few questions."

"Come back when we're not on break."

"Which is when?" Sadalia asked, becoming

more and more desperate. "I'm on deadline. This story goes to press in a few hours."

"That's too bad." The construction worker shrugged. "That's when we go back to work."

"Then what are you doing out here now?" Sadalia asked, not understanding her.

"Look," the construction worker said. She moved over on the edge of the fountain and patted a spot next to her. "You seem like a good kid. If we keep this short, we can have a chat. Take a seat."

Sadalia smiled and climbed off the fountain. Then she sat down next to the construction worker. *Now we're getting somewhere*, Sadalia thought. She took out her notepad and pencil, ready to write everything down.

The construction worker smiled and extended her right hand. "Name's Shorky. It's short for Shorkath, which isn't really much longer."

"Nice to meet you, Shorky," Sadalia said. "I thought I could maybe talk to you about some stuff."

"What kinda stuff you wanna talk about?" Shorky said, shifting her weight.

"Well, do you remember the dragon? From the other day?"

Shorky nodded. "You mean the *only* dragon from the other day? Yeah, I remember it. Why do you think there are so many of us working the graveyard shift? The cleanup for this is unbelievable. What about it?"

"I'm just wondering if you saw anything in the moments that led up to the appearance of the dragon. You were working in the area then, right?"

"Yeah, we were working. Unlike now," Shorky said, chuckling. "Anyway, there was nothing really unusual about the afternoon. It was pretty uneventful. We got hired to tear this fountain down, and someone decided to make it difficult."

"Who was it?" Sadalia asked.

Without skipping a beat, Shorky said, "It was Quest Guy."

"Quest Guy?" Sadalia asked as she wrote it down on her notepad.

"Yeah, Quest Guy. He was always messing stuff up for us with his antics. I hate antics," Shorky said, grumbling.

Quest Guy, Sadalia thought. *That's got to be Barley.*

"So this Quest Guy, what did he do that made life so difficult for you and your crew?" Sadalia asked.

"Well, you must have noticed that I used the past tense when I said, 'He WAS always messing stuff up.' I mean, you did notice, right? What with you being a reporter and all."

Sadalia scribbled on her notepad. "Oh, of course, yes. Totally noticed."

"Anyway," the construction worker continued, "we used to think he was just a big goofball. But it turns out that he knew exactly what he was talkin' about the whole time."

"So what did he do?" Sadalia said, dying to know.

"You wanna know what he did? I assume you do, which is why you asked in the first place. What he did was, he climbed to the top of the

fountain. Something about a kind of magic gem or something."

"Always talkin' about the old days, that history buff," added one of the other construction workers, a lanky cyclops who proceeded to shove half a sandwich in his mouth.

"Yeah, and to think we called the cops on him," Shorky continued. "At the time, we just thought, this guy is always keepin' us from our breaks."

"And our work," said the cyclops, with his mouth stuffed full of sandwich.

"Just the other day, for example," Shorky said, "Quest Guy was here. Tried to prevent us from tearing the fountain down to make way for condos. Said something about the place having 'historical value.'"

"Actually," said a troll construction worker, "he said, 'I won't let you tear it down! Ancient warriors on grand quests drank from this very fountain!'"

Shorky shot him a look. "Do I interrupt you when you're tellin' a story?"

"No, but that's 'cause you never let me tell a story," the troll replied.

"Yeah, I saw the video online," Sadalia interrupted. "These cops—do you remember their names?"

"Yeah, it was Gore and Specter," Shorky said.

Suddenly, Sadalia remembered seeing police activity near the fountain right before the curse destroyed the high school. She had completely forgotten about it since everything had unfolded so quickly. This must have been the piece of information that Gore and Specter hadn't wanted her to know.

"Wait, so getting back to the moment when Barley was climbing the fountain that night . . ." Sadalia said.

"Well, he did something to the fountain, and he pulled a glowing rock out of it," Shorky said. "We were all surprised. I mean, he had been right all along! The fountain *did* have historic value. There was a gem inside it after all!"

"Tell her about the red smoke," the cyclops

said, brushing sandwich crumbs from his shirt and mouth.

"Oh, that," Shorky said, almost like it was an afterthought. "Apparently, whatever Quest Guy did when he got his gem also unleashed a curse on our fair city. That must be part of the 'historic value.'"

"A curse?" Sadalia said, remembering what Shrub had told her before.

"A genuine, bona fide, one hundred percent, grade-A curse," Shorky said. "I know this, because that's what Quest Guy called it. And he seemed to know all about this kinda stuff. He's smart, that Quest Guy."

Sadalia was writing even faster now.

"So, this curse, it was like a big red cloud. It just started pourin' out of the fountain, like one of those, whaddaya call 'ems," Shorky said, turning to look at her fellow construction workers, snapping her fingers rapidly in succession.

"Geyser," said the troll.

"Geysers are water," Shorky grunted. "This wasn't no water."

"A blast?" offered the cyclops.

"Meh." Shorky shrugged.

The cyclops opened his mouth as if to say something, only to shove the other half of the sandwich inside.

"Anyway, red smoke came out of the fountain," Shorky said, dismissing the construction workers with her hand.

"The red smoke . . . did you see what happened to it?" Sadalia asked. She knew that it had to be the same red smoke that she had seen at the school, the smoke that somehow transformed the entire building into a dragon.

"Yeah," Shorky said. "It went that way." And she pointed toward the high school.

"Then what happened?" Sadalia asked.

"The red smoke, it goes all over the high school, see?" Shorky said. "Wrapping it up like a birthday present. And then the next thing I knew, POOF."

"Poof?" Sadalia said, writing it down.

"Yeah. POOF. The school was a dragon."

Now it was all beginning to make sense. The gem hidden inside the fountain was the Phoenix Gem. Ian and Barley's quest must have led them from the Path of Peril, back to the fountain, and to the hidden chamber atop the spire. Barley climbed the spire to get the Phoenix Gem, but in doing so, he accidentally unleashed a curse, which transformed the school into the dragon. Sadalia hadn't been in the town square when the curse was awoken, so she hadn't seen what Shorky was describing. But she *had* been outside the high school, and had witnessed the curse creating the dragon.

"Can you remember anything else, Shorky?" Sadalia said, standing up from her seat on the edge of the fountain.

"Nah," Shorky replied. "Just the school turning into a dragon. Darnedest thing I ever saw. Hey, guys, wasn't that the darnedest thing you ever saw?" Shorky said, slapping the arm of the cyclops construction worker.

They all nodded and murmured in agreement that it was, indeed, the darnedest thing that any of them had ever seen.

"And now, wouldn't you know it, it turns out the town is gonna save the fountain. It's gonna be a historic landmark. Quest Guy did it!" Shorky said, shaking her head.

"So you're not gonna tear it down?" Sadalia asked.

"No, I don't think we can get away with that," Shorky said. "Which is a shame, on account of I really like tearing stuff down. Ironic, considering our job is construction."

"Thanks for all your help," Sadalia said, extending her hand.

Shorky took it. "Pleasure was mine, kid. Good luck with your story."

Chapter 18

Dragons. Magic. Curses.

The words cascaded through Sadalia's mind as she practically sprinted away from the fountain. Up until this started, she'd thought those things were all in the past. Ancient artifacts, dusty relics that she'd only learned about in school.

But it turned out that they were all still very, very real.

From the edge of the park, she turned around, looking back at the fountain. It was hard to believe that just a short while ago, it had been home to a magic gem, and to an ancient curse.

Walking down the streets of New Mushroomton, Sadalia was busy figuring out her next move. There were still interviews that needed to be conducted, questions answered, and massive gaps in the story that needed to be filled.

But first, something wasn't sitting right with her. It was the whole part about Officer Gore saying she couldn't talk about what had happened at the fountain. Why couldn't she say anything? Did someone tell her not to? Did they know about the curse? Were they trying to keep things under wraps? Was there a cover-up going on, right beneath her nose? A . . . conspiracy?

The mere thought made Sadalia's head swim. The story was already big enough without thinking about all that. Plus, there were no facts to back up that theory. So she did what any good reporter would do. She made a mental note and vowed that she would look into it later. If the facts supported the theory, then she would follow them wherever they took her.

But right now, Sadalia realized that the best way to wrap up the loose ends of this story was to speak to Ian and Barley themselves. A real interview, not just a couple of minutes outside the high school before the cops whisked them away. Since they were at the police station, that might not be the easiest thing. She could easily walk inside the station, but getting the interview with Ian and Barley? That was going to be difficult.

Sadalia also still needed to interview Ian and Barley's mom, Laurel. She dreaded the awkwardness of showing up unannounced at the Lightfoot house at five in the morning, but it was her only option. She hoped Mrs. Lightfoot would understand once she knew Sadalia was trying to help Ian and Barley.

Deciding that was the next logical step, she pulled out her notebook. She checked through her notes and found the address of Ian and Barley's house: 313 Pennybun Lane. It was probably a fifteen-minute walk, she figured; Sadalia would be there in no time.

As she walked along the row of mushroom houses, Sadalia stopped at a red-capped house with a neat front yard and a basketball hoop over the garage. There were three news vans parked outside, with reporters milling around, waiting. They clutched microphones in their hands and paced back and forth, uneasy, impatient. Sadalia's heart sank a little. If the media were there, maybe they had already interviewed Laurel Lightfoot and were way ahead of Sadalia in getting the story.

She heard the little voice in her brain again, telling her that she might as well pack it in, that there was no point in pushing ahead with the story. *Let them take it from here,* the voice said. *Those reporters are professionals. REAL reporters. Not some kid working for her school paper.*

Maybe it was because she was so tired, but a part of Sadalia actually wanted to walk away, then and there, and head back home. She could potentially write a small piece that Mrs. Nightdale could run somewhere in the back of *The Fortnightly Dragon.*

Then there was another, louder voice. A voice that said NO.

So Sadalia pushed away the negative little voice in her mind. She wasn't going to give up that easily.

She flipped open her notebook and checked the address to make sure it matched her notes. Then she walked right past the reporters gathered by their vans and approached the door.

"Mrs. Lightfoot!" one reporter asked, chasing after Sadalia with her microphone.

"She's a kid. She's not Mrs. Lightfoot!" said another reporter.

"Greeb Sungrave, Channel Nine," said the third reporter as he pushed forward, microphone first. "WE want your story, and we're prepared to pay a very small amount of money to get it!"

"I'm not Mrs. Lightfoot," Sadalia said, trying to move around the reporter.

"Neither am I," Sungrave said, "but that's not going to stop me from getting the story of the century!"

Ugh, Sadalia thought. *Get in line. Everyone wants to get the story of the century. But you'll have to beat me to it!*

Sadalia pushed right past Greeb Sungrave and didn't break her stride. She simply walked up the path to the front door, climbed the steps, and rang the doorbell.

At least, she had been about to. The second before her finger could push the buzzer, Sadalia was greeted with roaring.

The sound was so unexpected that it caused her to leap backward. Then she heard a loud thump against the glass of the front window. Sadalia leaned over and saw the source of all the commotion. It was a small, scaly dragon.

The roars and yelps continued, but no one came to the front door. Figuring it wouldn't hurt to try, Sadalia rang the doorbell.

Still no response. So she rang the doorbell again. Nothing.

"She's not home!" called someone from the next yard over.

Sadalia turned her head and saw an older satyr standing by a large pot with only a single tiny flower in it. "Excuse me?"

"She's not home," the neighbor continued, watering the tiny flower. "Laurel. Mrs. Lightfoot. I already told those other people with their big hair and fancy vans. You'll have to come back later."

Sadalia backed away from the front door and the roaring dragon. Then she approached the neighbor. "Do you have any idea when she might be home?"

"None whatsoever," the woman said. "Trust me, if anyone would know, it would be me."

"Why's that?" Sadalia asked.

"Because I'm a busybody," the satyr replied. "Ask anybody around. They'll tell you. Name's Mrs. Grud."

"Thanks, Mrs. Grud," Sadalia said, disappointed. "I was really hoping to speak with Mrs. Lightfoot, but I guess I'll have to—"

"Have you tried the police station?" Mrs. Grud said. "I mean, it's pretty obvious you haven't, otherwise you'd be there right now. Laurel's probably there, bailing out her kids. Trust me, I'm a busybody."

Sadalia chuckled. "Yes, you mentioned that. I'm sorry, I didn't introduce myself. My name

187

is Sadalia Brushthorn. I'm a reporter with *The Fortnightly Dragon*. While I have you here, do you mind if I ask you a few questions?"

Mrs. Grud straightened, seeming to puff up a little. "A reporter, huh? I'm surprised you actually wanna talk to me."

"Why?" Sadalia asked, turning around to look at the other reporters assembled by their vans. "Didn't they interview you already?"

"Nah," Mrs. Grud said, waving her hand dismissively. "They think I'm just a chatterbox who doesn't know when to mind her own business, and to be fair, they're not wrong."

Sadalia watched as Mrs. Grud continued to water the already watered flower. "So, do you mind if I ask you some questions?" she asked again.

"Questions about what? 'Cause as long as we're talking about the people in this neighborhood, I'm pretty sure I'll have the answer."

"I'm betting that you watch people come and go around here all the time, don't you?"

Mrs. Grud nodded as she set the watering can

down on the lawn. "Sure do. All the time. It's a hobby. No, no . . . not a hobby . . . a vocation."

Sadalia smiled. "Did you happen to see the last time Ian and Barley left the house? Were they alone?"

Mrs. Grud pushed out her lower lip until her top lip sunk inward. Her gaze drifted upward as she started to think. "Hmmm. Yeah, I remember watching them leave. It was just the two of them, along with a pair of pants and some dress shoes."

Sadalia paused, realizing the significance of that comment. "These pants and shoes—"

"Dress shoes," Mrs. Grud insisted.

"Dress shoes," Sadalia repeated. She remembered something that Darmot, the former Manticore mascot turned sign twirler, had told her. "Did they walk around all by themselves?"

Mrs. Grud's eyes narrowed. "How did you know that?"

"Lucky guess," Sadalia said, glad to have confirmation that Darmot wasn't just seeing things.

"That's one lucky guess," Mrs. Grud said. "Anyway, yeah, those kids had these pants and dress shoes just walkin' around with them."

"You must have thought that was pretty strange," Sadalia said, making a note.

To her surprise, Mrs. Grud just shrugged. "Eh. When you've lived as long as I have, you've pretty much seen it all. Walking pants and dress shoes is the least of it. So I can't say I was really shocked by it."

"I guess not," Sadalia said.

"I mean, I'm nosy, right?" Mrs. Grud continued. "It's kinda my job to make note of all this stuff. I'm like the official historian of this neighborhood."

Sadalia suppressed a laugh. "Was there anything else?"

"Let's see," Mrs. Grud said, counting on the fingers of her right hand. "Laurel's not here, Ian and Barley are at the police station, and a walking pair of pants and dress shoes. Nope, that's about it."

"Thanks for your time!" Sadalia said, waving goodbye.

"Hey, when you write your story, make sure you spell my name right. It's spelled just like it sounds, G-R-U-D. Like MUD, with a GR. You'd be surprised how often people get it wrong."

Sadalia made sure to write it down. Just then, she heard the sound of a car pulling up in front of the Lightfoot house.

It was a police car.

Chapter 19

Sadalia's jaw practically dropped when she saw Mrs. Lightfoot get out of the car. She'd thought for sure that Ian and Barley's mom would still be at the police station. What was she doing home?

The reporters who were standing around their news vans suddenly came to life again, and there was a murmur of excitement in the crowd. They grabbed their microphones and raced toward the police car while their camera people struggled to keep up.

"Mrs. Lightfoot!" shouted one reporter.

"I'm with Channel Six Action News!" yelled another. "We want your story!"

The third reporter shoved a microphone in Mrs. Lightfoot's face and said, "Greeb Sungrave, Channel Nine. WE want your story, and we're prepared to pay a very small amount of money to get it!"

But it was clear that Mrs. Lightfoot wasn't having any of it. A hurried "No comment" was all she said while sprinting for the front door of her house.

Then a police officer got out of the car. He was huge, but moved quickly on his hooves, putting himself between Mrs. Lightfoot and the reporters. It was Officer Colt Bronco.

"She's not making any statements at this time," Officer Bronco said. He looked stern and strong, like he wasn't playing games. "Move aside, please. Official police business."

The reporters all groaned but did exactly as the officer ordered.

Sadalia stood on the lawn, watching Mrs. Lightfoot put her keys into the doorknob. Before she went inside, she looked over her shoulder, noticing Sadalia.

"Hello?" Mrs. Lightfoot said. "Ian's friend from school, right?"

Sadalia gulped. "Um, yeah," she said, suddenly

nervous. "Sadalia Brushthorn. I was just . . . how is Ian?"

Mrs. Lightfoot smiled. "Well, he'd be happy to know that somebody was asking how he was and not trying to make him pay to rebuild an entire school. Why don't you come in for a minute, Sadalia. It's a little too busy out here." Mrs. Lightfoot pointed at the reporters, who were standing just beyond the police officer, waving their microphones, now trying to get a statement out of *him.*

Unable to believe her good luck, Sadalia hurried across the lawn and up the steps to the Lightfoots' front door. Mrs. Lightfoot held it open, and Sadalia went inside.

The door closed, and Sadalia saw that Officer Bronco was now standing outside the front door to keep the reporters at bay.

"Where are Ian and Barley?" Sadalia asked.

"They're at the police station," Mrs. Lightfoot said, heading toward the kitchen.

Sadalia followed. "Are they in a lot of trouble?"

She had a ton of questions for Mrs. Lightfoot, but all she could think about was the boys right then, especially Ian.

Mrs. Lightfoot looked at Sadalia as she opened the refrigerator. "I'd say they're in the usual amount of trouble." Then she pulled a box out of the refrigerator and set it down on the kitchen table.

"What's that?" Sadalia asked.

"Cake. Ian's birthday cake. We never really got to celebrate, and I thought I could take it down to the police station so he could have some."

Sadalia was worried that Ian was going to be there for a long time. It must be so, otherwise he could just eat it when he got home.

"Mrs. Lightfoot," Sadalia said, feeling a little self-conscious, "don't you want to know why I'm here?"

"I know why you're here," Mrs. Lightfoot said, closing the refrigerator door. "You're worried about Ian."

"Yeah," Sadalia said. She was feeling a little guilty now. It's true that she was concerned about

Ian, but she *really* wanted to get her story. So she decided to be honest with Mrs. Lightfoot. "See, the thing is, I'm a—"

"Reporter for *The Fortnightly Dragon*, I know," Mrs. Lightfoot said, picking up the cake box from the table.

"Wait, how did you know?" Sadalia asked, surprised.

"Ian mentioned it to me. Plus, I've read some of your stories in the school paper. I thought your piece on traditional satyr dances was really well done."

Sadalia smiled. "Oh, thanks. I learned an awful lot while writing it."

"And now you're working on this story, huh?" Mrs. Lightfoot asked.

Sadalia nodded. "I just want everyone to know Ian and Barley's story, what they went through, and that they're just good people."

Mrs. Lightfoot put her arm around Sadalia. "Why don't you come down to the police station with me and Officer Bronco?"

"Do you mean it?" Sadalia said, hopeful. "I wouldn't be in the way or anything. And I promise to stop asking questions when you get tired of it."

Mrs. Lightfoot laughed. "Sounds like a deal."

When they left the house, Officer Bronco stretched out his arms, putting some distance between the reporters and Mrs. Lightfoot and Sadalia. They continued shouting questions, despite Officer Bronco's protests.

They finally made it to the car, and Officer Bronco opened the rear door for Sadalia. She got in the back and pulled out her notepad and pencil.

Mrs. Lightfoot and Officer Bronco got in, and the car pulled away from 313 Pennybun Lane.

"Laurel here tells me that you're a reporter for the school paper," Officer Bronco said.

"That's right," Sadalia said. "We actually met briefly the other day. I hope you don't mind if I ask some questions now."

"You can always ask," the police officer said.

"Whether I answer or not? Well, that's a different story."

Sadalia stared at Officer Bronco, not sure if he was kidding or being dead serious.

Then Mrs. Lightfoot punched his arm playfully. "Don't tease her like that, Colt."

Officer Bronco started to laugh. "Okay, okay. Go ahead, Sadalia. Hit us with your questions."

"Mrs. Lightfoot said that Ian and Barley were still at the police station. Why?"

"We brought them in for questioning, to help us piece together our report," Officer Bronco said. "So we could try to explain exactly what happened yesterday. I don't know if you noticed, but it was a little, shall we say, unusual."

"That's one way to put it," Sadalia said. "And Mrs. Lightfoot also mentioned something about Ian having to pay for all the damage?"

"Oh yeah," Officer Bronco said, nodding. "There's been a lot of talk about holding somebody responsible. Me? I'd have gone after the dragon, but considering the dragon is now a big pile of bricks, that's not gonna work. So just in case, we've been making Ian and Barley keep a low profile. Figured that was better than them facing a whole town full of questions and bills for damage. Those reporters back there? That's just the tip of the iceberg."

"Then they're not in trouble?" Sadalia asked.

Officer Bronco chuckled. "No more than usual. I'd say it's the perfect amount of trouble."

"So if they're not going to jail, does that mean that they're—"

"Heroes," Laurel said proudly. "That's what they are. Heroes."

"It's a little more complicated than that, honey," Officer Bronco added. "But they did a good thing. And so did you," he said to Laurel.

"Yeah, about that, Mrs. Lightfoot. I saw you at the school when it became a dragon and all. What was your part in all of this?"

Mrs. Lightfoot turned around so she could see Sadalia. "Who, me? Don't you want to talk to Ian and Barley? I'm sure they can tell you more than I can. I was just an innocent bystander."

"Well, from where I was sitting, you were an innocent bystander wielding a sword, teaming up with the Manticore to help vanquish a dragon," Sadalia said.

Officer Bronco pumped his fist and cheered, "Laurel Lightfoot, the mighty warrior!"

"Oh, stop, Colt," Mrs. Lightfoot said. "There's not much to the story, Sadalia. I came back home and knew that something was wrong when I saw that Ian's usually perfect room was a complete mess. He's kind of a neat freak. No way he'd leave his room like that. Then I found one of Barley's game cards for the Manticore's Tavern nearby, so I knew they must have headed there. And when I arrived, the Manticore told me about the curse and how the boys were totally unaware of it. I couldn't let them deal with that on their own. What kind of mom would I be?"

"And so the two of you went to the pawn shop to get the Curse Crusher, right?" Sadalia asked. "That's the sword you were using to battle the dragon?"

"Yes, and that scoundrel of an owner tried to

swindle us, so the Manticore took matters into her own hands. Lucky she did, or I don't think we would have made it in time."

"I have to say—I thought you were awesome during the battle. The dragon never saw you coming," Sadalia said.

"What else could I do? I had to help my boys."

Sadalia slid back in her seat in the police cruiser. Her mind was in overdrive. All the parts of the story were coming together, and she was on her way to getting an exclusive interview with Ian and Barley that would make everything complete. She was writing down notes as fast as she could, hoping she hadn't missed anything.

But stray thoughts kept popping up. Like that pair of pants, for instance. Obviously, pairs of pants don't just walk around by themselves. Somebody was wearing those pants. But were they invisible? Magic could do that, right?

It had to be Shades, she thought—it had to be! Maybe that's why Shades was all bundled up . . . because he actually didn't have a top half!

Whatever Ian and Barley—especially Barley—did, they had unleashed the curse on the town. But they were also instrumental in stopping it. They had the help of the Manticore and Laurel. Both were wielding the Curse Crusher sword, whose name suddenly made a lot more sense to Sadalia.

So where did Shades fit into all this? Sadalia wondered if the Phoenix Gem had something to do with it. Ian and Barley needed the Phoenix Gem, which was why they went on their quest in the first place, why they traversed the Path of Peril. Maybe they needed it to help Shades?

If that was the case, they had *gone* to an awful lot of trouble, *caused* an awful lot of trouble, and gotten *into* an awful lot of trouble. She felt like she had almost all the information. Now all she needed was Ian and Barley to confirm it.

Sadalia looked at her phone to check the time. "Chantar's Talon!"

"What? What's wrong?" Officer Bronco exclaimed.

"Oh, sorry," Sadalia said, realizing her outburst had come out of nowhere. "It's almost six a.m.? That can't be the time!"

But when she looked out the window, her eyes confirmed it. The sun was rising—morning was already there! That wasn't how it was supposed to go! She should have finished all the interviews and been at home by then, finishing at *least* the second or third draft of her story.

But there she was, not even remotely close to starting the *first* draft.

If she asked Officer Bronco to drop her off at home, she might be able to write the story. But even if she did, the story would be incomplete. It wouldn't be as good as it could be if she had the interviews with Ian and Barley. And how would she address the questions that lingered? There were still massive dragon-sized holes in her story.

Which meant it wouldn't be the story that she needed it to be. And she could forget about that editor in chief spot the next year. She was certainly certain about that.

"Mrs. Nightdale told me she needed the story by the morning," Sadalia said. "That means I have until journalism class. That's ten a.m. So I've got a couple hours to pull this off."

Officer Bronco shook his head. "I think you've been so focused on your story that you're missing the obvious. There isn't a school left to go to today."

"So okay, there won't be any school today, but Mrs. Nightdale said that the paper would be printed as usual," Sadalia insisted. "She said it was even *more* important to report the news at a time like this."

"It's certainly been an . . . unusual time," Officer Bronco said reassuringly. "But I don't think the school will resume printing the paper for at least a few days. Mrs. Nightdale may have gotten a little ahead of herself."

"But why wasn't I told? I haven't heard anything!"

"Probably because you've been out all night pursuing your story. When something this big happens, you have to imagine the effect that it has. The school was destroyed, so it had to be shut down. We need a few days to put emergency plans into action. So school is canceled until the plans can be worked out. That means no after-school activities, too. And no school paper. The police coordinated with the superintendent of schools, and we helped notify everyone in the school system."

"So . . . there's no school. I have more time for my story!"

"That's it in a nutshell," Officer Bronco said with a grin.

Chapter 20

When they arrived at the police station, Officer Bronco told Sadalia to go right in. "Just tell the officer at the front desk that I sent you, and they'll take you back to Ian and Barley."

"Wait," Sadalia said. "Why aren't you going inside with me? Mrs. Lightfoot?"

"We'll be right there," Mrs. Lightfoot said. "We have one quick stop to make, and we'll be right back."

Sadalia stepped out of the police cruiser and shut the door. She paused for just a moment outside the police station, then ran up the steps and threw open the front door. She couldn't believe that after two days of nonstop chasing and interviewing she'd finally be talking to Ian and Barley themselves.

"Let's have it again," the desk officer said. "One more time, from the top."

"I'm a reporter from *The Fortnightly Dragon*," Sadalia said to the desk officer for what seemed like the tenth time. She was resting both hands on the officer's high desk, looking up, trying desperately not to roll her eyes. "And I need to see Ian and Barley Lightfoot. Officer Colt Bronco sent me and told me to tell you that it's okay for me to be here."

"That's a no-can-do," the desk officer said, scratching his chin, pulling at a few wiry whiskers. "I can neither confirm nor deny that *either* of those people are presently within the confines of this establishment."

"That's okay, she's with me," came a voice from behind as Sadalia felt a heavy hand rest upon her shoulder.

"Officer Specter?"

Sadalia couldn't believe it. Was Officer Specter actually . . . helping her?

"You know this person?" the desk officer asked.

"Of course I know her," Officer Specter said. "She's Sadalia Brushthorn with *The Fortnightly Dragon*. We go way back."

"Yesterday counts as 'way back'?" Sadalia whispered.

"Just go with it, kid," Specter said.

"Well, if you can vouch for her," the desk officer said, shrugging his shoulders. "You know, she's a reporter for that school newspaper."

"I just said that," Officer Specter replied. "I'll take her back with me." She put her arm around Sadalia. The desk officer waved at them as they walked through a waist-high wooden gate.

Sadalia turned to Officer Specter. "I thought for sure I wouldn't get in. Thank you. But . . . why *did* you let me in?"

At first, Officer Specter didn't say anything. She just kept walking until they came to a door at the end of the hallway. Specter reached down to her belt, tugging on a keyring connected to an elastic cord. She fumbled briefly with the keyring until she found a tarnished brass key and used it to unlock the door. It opened with a creak, and Specter motioned for Sadalia to walk inside.

As they went along the corridor, they passed by a number of offices. Finally, they came to one with the name COLT BRONCO on the door.

"Because I like you, Sadalia," Officer Specter said. "Now get in there and get your interview."

Sadalia gulped, then opened the door and saw two boys lounging on the couch.

"Sadalia!" Ian exclaimed. "What are you doing here?"

"I'm doing my job," Sadalia said with conviction. "I'm gonna write the story for *The Fortnightly Dragon* that tells everyone what you two did. When I'm done, everyone's gonna know that you and your brother are heroes."

Standing in Officer Bronco's office, Sadalia suddenly had a strange feeling come over her. It was as if all the questions she had wanted to ask Ian and Barley seemed to abandon her all at once. She was sitting with the Lightfoot brothers, who were at the epicenter of the most epic thing to ever happen in town, and Sadalia couldn't think of a single thing to say.

"That sure was something, wasn't it?" Barley said to Sadalia. "You ever seen anything like that before?"

"No," Sadalia said, shaking her head. "I . . ."

"Yeah?" Ian said. "Sadalia, are you okay?"

"Ian . . ." Sadalia said, searching for the words. "I have to know, what was this all about? I pieced so much of it together, and I think I have an idea, but I don't know everything."

"What do you want to know?" Ian asked.

"Shades," Sadalia blurted out. "That's not my name for him, that was from Dewdrop, the Pixie Duster."

"You met the Pixie Dusters?" Ian asked. "And you're still here?"

Sadalia laughed. "Yeah, I met Dewdrop. She wasn't that bad. We bonded over being fellow motorcycle and scooter enthusiasts."

Ian and Barley looked impressed.

"So, Shades. Was it the same person who was

pretending to be Ian when Officers Gore and Specter pulled the van over? And why was Officer Bronco there?"

Ian and Barley glanced at each other. Then they looked over Sadalia's shoulder at the open office door.

Standing there was Officer Bronco. He glared at the boys.

"About that . . ." Ian started to say.

"Yes, Ian," Officer Bronco said. "About that. Why don't you tell the young lady exactly what happened. Start from the beginning, because this is good."

"But first," Mrs. Lightfoot said, looking over Officer Bronco's shoulder, "birthday cake!"

She walked into the office and set the birthday cake that she'd picked up from her house down on the desk. Then she pulled a handful of candles out of a small bag.

"Colt and I made a special trip to get these candles," she said. "It was hard finding a place open this early."

Mrs. Lightfoot produced a book of matches from her pocket and then lit the candles. "Happy Birthday, Ian! You sure do deserve it."

Then the group all wished Ian a happy birthday.

"Who wants cake?" Mrs. Lightfoot said. "Do you want some, Sadalia?"

"Thanks, Mrs. Lightfoot," Sadalia said, "but I think if I tried to eat right now, I'd throw up. And isn't it a little early for cake?"

"It's never too early for cake," Barley said, cutting himself a big slice.

Once they had filled themselves with cake, Officer Bronco, Mrs. Lightfoot, and Barley left the office to grab coffee, leaving Sadalia with Ian.

"So what can you tell me about you and Barley? How did all this come about?"

Ian rocked back and forth for a moment. "My brother and I . . . we've always been really different from each other. I love my brother, but we are definitely NOT the same person."

"Yeah, I saw the video of him at the fountain," Sadalia said. "You are *definitely* different."

Ian smiled. "That's my brother. Not afraid to put himself out there. Never has been. He rushes right into the world, and doesn't change who he is or anything about himself for anyone. I really admire that."

"Is that why you invited me to your birthday party?" Sadalia asked. "Was that your way of putting yourself out there?"

Ian nodded. "Yeah, that's right. My mom suggested the party, actually. And the more I thought about it, I realized she was right. No one really knows me. I just kind of keep to myself, or I hang out with Kagar. Don't get me wrong, Kagar is awesome, but . . ."

"But you need people to see you," Sadalia said.

"Yeah, exactly."

"That's what this story's going to do," Sadalia said. "Tell everyone who you are, in your own words."

Suddenly, there was a knock at the door, and Barley poked his head in. "Hey! I brought you a

cup of hot chocolate," he said, handing one to Ian. "And one for you, Sadalia."

"Thanks," Sadalia said.

"Barley, you're a part of this, too," Ian said, pulling up a chair for his brother.

Barley eagerly sat down. He didn't seem to notice that he had a big hot chocolate mustache across his upper lip.

"Finally! Let's do this," Barley said.

"Yeah," Ian echoed. "Let's do this."

Chapter 21

"**I**t was Sir Iandore Lightfoot's sixteenth birthday," Barley began. "You know, in the days of old, an adventurer of that age would have had his strength tested in the Swamps of Despair."

"I didn't know that," Sadalia said.

It was quiet for a moment, then Ian spoke. "You know that we lost our father, right?"

"I knew, but I didn't know," Sadalia said. "Does that make sense?"

Ian nodded. "Barley at least knew our dad. I never met him. He passed away before I was born."

Barley smiled. "I knew him, but I was really little. Like, three years old. I only had a few memories of him." He started to count on his fingers. "I remembered he had a scratchy beard. And that he had this really loud, goofy laugh. And I used to play drums on his feet."

Barley moved his hands over Officer Bronco's desk and rapped his knuckles on its surface five times. Then he blew two raspberries to punctuate the drumming.

"That was it," Barley said.

"I do have a tape recording of him and Mom," Ian said quietly. "I've listened to it so many times I've memorized the conversation. Sometimes . . . sometimes I would even pretend that I was talking to him."

Sadalia nodded.

Ian cleared his throat. "So, it was my birthday, and . . . just once, you know, I wished that I could spend the day with my dad. Just once. But that wasn't something that was ever going to happen."

"Or so you thought!" Barley interjected.

Sadalia's eyes went wide. "Excuse me? Are you . . . are you suggesting what I think you're suggesting?"

"Let's not get ahead of ourselves," Ian said. "Barley likes to do that. Anyway, Mom gave me a present for my birthday. Actually, it was from

Dad. Something that he had left for me and for Barley to open. When we were both over sixteen."

"What was it?" Sadalia asked.

"It was—" Ian began.

"A WIZARD STAFF!" Barley shouted. "Can you believe it? A real wizard staff! Not some cheapo toy wizard staff, like the ones you can get at Journey Mart."

"It was our dad's," Ian said. "Because he was a wizard. He wrote a letter to both of us."

"It contained a Visitation Spell," Barley added. "A spell to bring someone back, but only for one day. There was a Phoenix Gem wrapped up with the staff. That's—"

"An assist element," Sadalia finished. "It's what you need to make a powerful spell work."

"Yeah, that's right!" Barley said, impressed. "So I put the Phoenix Gem at the top of the wizard staff. Then I said the spell."

"Did it work?" Sadalia said, hanging on every word.

"Not so much," Barley said. "So I tried it again.

219

And again. And again. And again. Couldn't make anything happen."

"So what did you do?" Sadalia asked.

"It's not what I did," Barley said. "It's what *he* did." And then he pointed at Ian.

Ian nodded. "Guilty as charged."

"Don't say 'guilty' in a police station," Barley said. "That's bad luck!"

"And then you brought your dad back!" Sadalia exclaimed.

"Yes," Ian said. "And no."

Barley settled in his chair and looked at Sadalia. "What we're about to tell you isn't for the faint of heart. Even the bravest warrior wouldn't be prepared for the shock we received."

"The shock? The shock of what?"

"So the spell did work, but only partway," Barley said. "All we brought back of Dad was his pants and shoes."

The last big piece clicked into place for Sadalia in that moment. "So Shades was your dad! And he was actually just a pair of pants!"

"Yes, that was him," Ian said. "The spell was too powerful, so the Phoenix Gem exploded before the spell could finish. The gem shattered into a thousand pieces. Blew out the window to my bedroom."

"So after all that, you only got to spend a day with half of your dad?" Sadalia said. "That's so sad."

"Well, it wasn't entirely sad," Ian said. "In fact, it ended up not being sad at all."

"Because we had a quest to undertake!" Barley exclaimed.

"The Phoenix Gem," Sadalia said. "That's why you needed to get another Phoenix Gem. Because the first one was destroyed, and you needed a new one to complete the Visitation Spell."

Barley nodded.

"So you took Barley's van on the quest," Sadalia said.

"Guinevere," Barley said. "Guinevere's my van. Well, she *was* my van."

"Was?" Sadalia asked.

"Barley sacrificed her when we were on the Path of Peril," Ian said. "The cops were chasing after us, so he used her to block the path. It was only because of Barley that we made it as far as we did."

"Now she has ascended to the halls of Valhalla!" Barley said. "She was a good girl."

"So *that's* why I couldn't make it through!" Sadalia exclaimed. "I followed the path, but it was totally blocked by an avalanche."

Ian and Barley stared at her. "You went on the Path of Peril alone?" Ian asked.

"Yeah, of course," Sadalia replied.

"You pursued this quest with the fortitude of a warrior," Barley said. "Or maybe the cleverness of a rogue."

"It was more of an investigation than a quest," Sadalia said.

"An in-questigation!" Barley exclaimed, clearly pleased with his play on words.

Sadalia smiled. She liked Barley already. But she still had questions. "One thing I'm not getting . . . you used your dad's spell to bring him back, almost by accident. You didn't know what you were doing."

Ian nodded. "Not at all. I just happened to recite the spell because, why not? What did I have to lose?"

"But it worked," Sadalia said, looking at him. "It *worked*."

"Yeah . . ." Ian said. "What are you getting at?"

"Well, how did you learn magic so quickly? It's like you just became a wizard overnight!"

Barley turned to face Sadalia, and he wagged his index finger. "He didn't *become* a wizard. No, no. He was *born* a wizard."

"Well, I had a lot of help from Barley," said Ian. "He knows everything about magic."

"I helped a bit," said Barley, "but it's said that a person can only do magic if they have the gift. And guess who has it? The magic gift?" Then he jabbed a finger in Ian's direction repeatedly.

"But how did you learn everything so quickly?" Sadalia asked.

"That's easy," Barley said. "With this."

He held aloft the *Quests of Yore* player's guide and tossed it on the desk in front of Sadalia. She picked up the book and opened it. Thumbing through the volume, she saw page after page of characters, relics, and spells—a world of fantastic magic.

"It's historically accurate," Barley said. "Even the spells. That's why I gave it to Ian and told him to practice."

"And I needed the practice," Ian said. "Later on, when we ran out of gas, I tried to do the Growth Spell to grow more gas. I shrank Barley instead."

A realization dawned on Sadalia: the security tape. "Wait, is that why Barley was so tiny at the gas station? I watched the security footage and saw that you could fit in Ian's pocket! I thought I was seeing things."

Barley and Ian burst out laughing. "Yeah, that was real, all right," said Barley. "What a crazy night that was. The sprites chased us, so Ian had

to drive Guinevere. We barely made it out of there."

"It wasn't funny at the time because I thought we were gonna die," Ian added. "But now it sounds totally insane."

Barley ruffled Ian's hair. "But we lived to tell the tale! And then right after that, Ian had to use the Disguise Spell because Gore and Specter pulled us over. Thankfully, I had grown back by that point, but my wallet hadn't. So we were gonna get caught without our licenses. They saw Colt on the road, but the *real* Colt was nowhere near the area. It was actually *us* in disguise! Ian was the front and I was the back. We had to do it to keep Dad from getting arrested."

"I knew it!" Sadalia exclaimed. "Your dad was the one in the puffy clothes, but the police thought he was Ian. Very clever."

"We thought so, too," said Barley.

"But I'm still not understanding how Ian suddenly got so good at casting spells by the time he fought the dragon," Sadalia said. "Because from what I saw, you looked like a pro. What's the secret?"

Barley and Ian looked at her strangely. "Secret?" Ian asked.

"The secret is . . . you have to speak from your Heart's Fire," Barley said. "And before you say, 'WHAT'S THAT?' I'll tell you what it is. Your Heart's Fire means you have to speak with passion. You can't hold anything back."

"I didn't know what my Heart's Fire was at first," said Ian. "It took me a while to find it."

Sadalia had one final question, but it was the one thing she was most nervous to ask about. "So . . ." she began, "what ended up happening with your dad? Did you finish the spell? In the chaos of the battle, I didn't see what happened."

Ian and Barley looked at each other, exchanging sad smiles. "Ian made the ultimate sacrifice," said Barley. "He gave up his chance to meet Dad so I could say goodbye."

Sadalia didn't know what to say. Ian was the

one to break the silence. "The dragon was coming after us. Someone needed to distract it. And Barley deserved his chance to say goodbye to Dad. It took this quest for me to realize—I never had a dad, but I always had *Barley*."

Chapter 22

Sadalia had nearly everything she needed for her story. Even with all her theories, she would have never guessed that Ian and Barley's quest was all a result of wanting to see their father. Sadalia couldn't think of a better reason for this adventure.

Despite her lack of sleep, she was feeling good. Inspired, even. That all changed when she finally noticed there was a circular clock on the wall next to the door, and that the clock said it was 7:42 a.m. By now, her parents would've realized she'd snuck out.

"I am so dead," Sadalia said, not realizing she was actually speaking out loud.

"You seem pretty alive to me. Unless you're some kind of undead creature risen from the grave," Barley joked.

"No, I'm *really* dead. I have to let my parents know where I am! They already grounded me for being out so late last night."

"Maybe Colt could—"

"What's that now?" said Officer Bronco.

Everyone turned toward the door to see the police officer standing in the doorway with Laurel.

"Maybe you could help Sadalia get out of trouble with her parents?" Ian suggested.

"Already done," said Officer Bronco. "I called Sadalia's parents and told them that she was a key witness in 'The Incident' and we needed to get a statement from her. And I said we stopped by the house very, very early and gave her a ride to the station." Then he raised an eyebrow.

"You . . . you did that for me?" Sadalia said, incredulous.

"He did," Laurel said. "I know you're doing your part to write a story telling the town about my boys and what they did. It seemed the least we could do for you."

"I . . . I don't know what to say," Sadalia said. "Thank you."

"You're welcome," Officer Bronco said, tipping his hat.

Sadalia laughed. "I can't believe my luck. But what I really can't believe is that you brought magic back to the world," she said, pointing at Ian. "You did. You, the kid who invited me to his house for a party and then turned around a minute later and disinvited me."

"In all fairness, it was at least a couple of minutes later," Ian said. "Anyway, I don't think we brought magic back. Not really. It's more like it was always with us, all around us. We just . . . we just reminded everyone about it."

"He totally brought it back," Barley said, dismissing Ian's humble words.

Laurel beamed at her two sons. "Your father would be so proud. I'm so proud of you both."

"So am I," Officer Bronco said. "Even if officially I have to 'come down' on you for 'destroying the school.'" He looked around at the sleep-deprived group. "I think it's time we wrap things up and head home. It's been a long couple days. What do you say, Sadalia?"

When Sadalia stopped to think about it, she was truly exhausted. She couldn't wait to get home. "I think that sounds like a good idea, Officer Bronco. But do you think I could get a ride home? I couldn't borrow my mom's minivan, and my scooter completely died on me. I guess it's trash now." Then she looked at Ian. "Unless you know a spell that can repair it."

Ian smiled. "I'm sure I could figure out something."

"That takes care of that particular problem," Officer Bronco said. "Now we just have to figure out what we're going to do with you two."

"Wait." Sadalia jumped up. "I thought you said they weren't in trouble! That they weren't going to jail!"

"They're not going to jail," Officer Bronco said. "But trouble? They're already neck-deep in that. They were responsible for the destruction of public property, including and not limited to the high school. I've already had phone calls—screaming phone calls—from the school, the school district, parents. Do you have any idea how much my ears hurt from all the screams?"

"A lot?" Sadalia said.

"A lot," Officer Bronco replied. "See the cotton in these ears?" He showed Sadalia the little wad of cotton in each ear. "The only reason I have any hearing left whatsoever is because of this. So we have to figure out something, some way for the boys to make some kind of restitution for the destruction, even if they didn't intend for any of it to happen."

"I'm sorry about the dragon and the school being destroyed," Ian said. "But I wouldn't change any of it. Not one thing."

"Spoken like a true adventurer," Barley said.

"I wouldn't change a thing, either," Laurel agreed.

Officer Bronco nodded. "Neither would I. Except for maybe the people screaming at me."

The room grew quiet. Then it hit her.

"Magic," Sadalia said. Everyone in the room turned to look at her. "The answer is *magic.*"

"What are you saying?" Ian asked.

"You, Ian," Sadalia continued. "You and your gift. The magic gift. Couldn't you use your magic to rebuild the school? I mean, if magic was responsible for changing bricks and mortar into a fire-breathing dragon, and magic turned the dragon back into bricks and mortar, then couldn't magic reorganize and rearrange the bricks and mortar to remake the school?"

"That . . . that's not a terrible idea," Officer Bronco said.

"That's an amazing idea," Barley said. "We could do it! YOU could do it!" He slapped his brother on the back, hard.

"Ow," Ian said.

"Sure," Sadalia said. "If you could use a spell to repair my scooter, couldn't you also use a spell to rebuild the school?"

"Maybe," Ian said. "Maybe," he repeated, his

voice sounding more excited. "That might work! Barley, do you think that would work?"

"Fear not, little brother!" Barley exclaimed in a deep voice. "Between us, we shall reconstruct the School of Destiny!" He paused. "But the question is: which spells will do the trick? Oooh, I may need to gather the fellowship. I think if we all put our heads together, we can figure it out. Shrub will have some ideas for sure. We probably won't be able to shut him up once I tell him."

"Boys, if you can pull this off, that would go a long way toward satisfying Principal Pipplemell's call for revenge," Officer Bronco said.

Sadalia's jaw dropped slightly. "Did Principal Pipplemell really call for revenge?"

"She said, and I quote, 'Mark my words, Officer Bronco. Those Lightfoot boys will feel my wrath and feast upon my vengeance. For what they've done to my beloved school, they will know the pain of the elders!'"

"Did she really say all that?" Laurel said, recoiling a little.

Officer Bronco nodded. "She was very specific."

"Yikes," Sadalia said. "Better get on that spell, Ian."

A short while later, Sadalia was standing outside the police station, waiting for Officer Bronco to come out and give her a ride home. She was glad to be outside and have a few minutes alone to collect her thoughts. The past couple of days had been unlike anything she had ever experienced, and her reporter's brain was trying to process everything.

On the one hand, she was relieved that she had gotten a reprieve on the story. Knowing that school was canceled until further notice and that she had a few days' grace on turning in her article helped a little. It would give her some time to set down all the information on paper, collect her thoughts, conduct some follow-up interviews if she needed to, and then start writing.

She looked out toward the road. A car

approached, and Sadalia noticed the driver was Shorky, the construction worker she had been talking to just a few hours earlier. Sadalia waved, and Shorky waved back.

"I thought you had to work this morning," Sadalia called out as Shorky stopped the car in front of the police station.

"This is me working," Shorky said. "You get all your answers?"

Sadalia nodded. "Not all, but most."

"Well, that's more than most of us get," Shorky said. "Look, you ever want a job in the construction industry, you come see me, okay? I could use someone like you."

"Will do," Sadalia said, and she waved once more as Shorky drove off. Sadalia looked up at the morning sun and sighed.

"Hey," came a voice from behind her. Sadalia looked over her shoulder and saw Ian walk out the front door of the police station.

"Hey," she replied. "Came to see me off?"

"I just wanted to say thanks for helping Barley

and me," Ian said. "I appreciate how hard you're working to clear our names. I just hope all this magic stuff didn't weird you out. I guess this is what happens when you hang out with a wizard. I mean, if you want to hang out with a wizard."

"Yeah, of course I want to hang out with a wizard! How cool is that?" Sadalia said. "Thanks, Ian."

"For what?" he said.

"For everything," Sadalia said. "For the interview. For opening my eyes. I always heard about magic, and knew it was something that had existed, but it was like a fairy tale. You know, something so far removed that it might as well not be real. But you showed me that there is magic in the world. It sounds corny, I know, but . . . maybe people need more of that."

"Maybe they do," Ian said.

They sat back down on the steps of the police station, looking out where the school once stood.

"Now you just have to rebuild an entire school," Sadalia said.

Ian laughed. "Yeah. That'll be some trick."

"Thanks for sharing your story with me," Sadalia said.

Ian smiled. "Did I tell you about the booby traps?"

"Booby traps!" Sadalia exclaimed. "There were booby traps?"

"They were only some of the most frightening things I've ever seen in my life. We had reached this place that Barley called the Final Gauntlet. . . ."

Sadalia and Ian sat on the steps while he regaled her with more stories from his quest.

"Sadalia! Are you awake?"

"Huh?"

It was her mom calling up the stairs.

"I am now," Sadalia said, sitting up in bed with a start. She ran her hands through her hair and blinked several times, trying to wake up.

"Then come on down, please. Someone's here to see you."

"Someone's here to see me?" Sadalia said as she shuffled her feet along the carpet and through her doorway into the hall. Walking down the stairs, she was surprised to see Ian standing in the kitchen.

"Ian?" Sadalia said. "What are you doing here? I just left you at the police station. I thought for sure you'd still be there."

"That was yesterday," he said. "Have you been asleep since you got home?"

Sadalia's mom smiled. "As a matter of fact, she has been asleep for the last twenty-four hours. Anyway, it was nice to meet you, Ian. Sadalia, I'll be in the living room. Holler if you need anything."

"Thanks, Mom," Sadalia said as her mother left the kitchen. She sat down at the table and motioned for Ian to join her.

"Sorry, I'm a little fuzzy around the edges right now," Sadalia said. "I meant to start working on the story when I got home, but I couldn't keep my eyes open. I just sort of hit the bed, and the

next thing I know, my mom's calling me and now you're here."

"Yeah, I had the same problem," Ian said. "When I finally got home, I went straight to bed. Next thing I knew, it was today."

"So what brings you here?" Sadalia asked.

"I was giving it a lot of thought and . . . I think your piece should focus on Barley. He's the true hero of the story."

Sadalia was surprised. "Yeah, but *you* were the one who could perform magic. You brought your dad back!"

"I know," Ian said. "But I couldn't have done any of it without Barley. He's taken care of me, encouraged me, pushed me to be a better person. It's because of him that I even believed in myself enough to learn magic. And this whole experience has made me realize that all the stuff that I've been holding on to, all the thoughts and feelings and stuff I used to believe just because this inner voice in my head kept telling me it was true, all of that—I need to let it go, you know? And that only happened because of Barley."

Sadalia looked away. She knew exactly what he meant. Her inner voice had been telling her that it was too hard to be a reporter—that it wouldn't work, that she wasn't good enough. It had taken the events of the past two days for her to tell the voice to back off, that she wasn't going to stop, and that she was going to achieve her dreams no matter what.

Sadalia hesitated for a moment before asking her next question. "What did your dad say to Barley when he was fully conjured? You don't have to tell me if it's too personal."

Ian chuckled. "He told Barley that he'd hoped his wizard name would be Wilden the Whimsical."

"That's an . . . interesting name," Sadalia said.

"It's terrible!" Ian replied. "He also said that he was very proud of me, of the person I had grown up to be."

"Did he say anything else?"

"No," Ian said, casting his eyes down at his feet. "He just told Barley to give me a hug."

"You're lucky to have a brother like him," Sadalia said.

"Yeah," Ian said, and then he thought for a moment. "I don't know why it took me so long to realize it. Of course, I'll always want to meet Dad, but I spent all those years wishing for him and never saw what I had right in front of me: Barley."

Sadalia nodded. "I'll make sure everyone knows about Barley. But I think you were kinda important, too. I'll write about both of you, but I think when I'm done, everyone will know that Barley is a lot more than 'Quest Guy.'"

"Who's Quest Guy?" Ian asked.

Sadalia laughed. "Kind of a long story."

EPILOGUE

A couple of weeks had passed since the Day the School Turned into a Dragon. Nobody could think of a better name for it, so that's the name that had taken hold. Sadalia thought it was too long and not very catchy, but it didn't seem to bother anyone else.

New Mushroomton High School was still closed. The students had been reassigned to various schools within the area. Classes were split up, but the students adapted and did their best with what they had.

All the clubs and activities still went on as usual. The same went for *The Fortnightly Dragon*. Sadalia had surprised herself and Mrs. Nightdale by turning in her story only a few days after the event itself. She called it "The Search for the Phoenix Gem." Mrs. Nightdale had thought for sure that Sadalia would need more time to work on it, but Sadalia was like a person possessed. Once she started writing, the words wouldn't stop coming.

That's what happens when you tap into your Heart's Fire, Sadalia thought.

Now the story was out there for all of New Mushroomton to read. Mrs. Nightdale told her that the papers had been flying off the shelves like never before. She said that the editor in chief spot was Sadalia's the next year—if she wanted it. Which Sadalia totally and completely did. Though she was happy about the recognition, Sadalia realized that writing about the truth and getting it out there for the realm to read was all the reward she needed.

She was walking down the corridor of her temporary school when she spied Ian and Kagar coming her way. To her surprise, Ian was reading a copy of her article as he walked.

"Hey," Sadalia said, right before Ian practically

walked right into her. "Hard to read while you walk!"

"Hey, Sadalia," Ian said. "I'm sorry, I didn't see you standing there. I was just reading your story."

"It's *your* story," Sadalia said. "Yours and Barley's. I just happened to be in the right place at the right time."

"It's amazing," Kagar said, grabbing the paper from Ian's hands. "This part here, when they were on the Path of Peril—I couldn't believe it. So dramatic! Especially the part about crossing the Bottomless Pit."

"That *was* actually pretty dramatic," Ian said.

Sadalia nodded. "I can confirm that, considering I thought my minivan was going to fall right in."

"I guess you guys are pretty much heroes," Kagar said. "You and Barley. Except for causing the school to turn into a dragon. That, not so much."

"Hey, let's be clear, I didn't *personally* turn

the school into a dragon," Ian said. "That was the curse's fault."

"Uh-huh," Kagar said. "And who unleashed the curse?"

Ian mumbled something, but neither Kagar nor Sadalia could hear him.

"I'm sorry, what was that?" Kagar said.

"I did," Ian said in a voice just below a whisper.

"What?" Kagar repeated.

"I DID," Ian said loudly, causing the other students passing by to turn their heads and stare. Ian lowered his voice. "But Barley and I are working hard to rebuild the school. I think we've just cracked the spells we'll need. It'll require a lot of concentration and energy on my part, but I'm pretty confident that this will work."

Sadalia smiled. "Well, if all this hadn't happened, then people would have just forgotten about the old days, like they had never existed. And they wouldn't know what you sacrificed to save everyone that day."

"I guess," Ian said. "I'm just glad that everything worked out."

"It only worked out because of you and Barley," Sadalia said. "And your dad."

"And Dad," Ian echoed.

The school bell rang, and Kagar raced off to class with a wave.

"See you after school?" Ian asked.

"That's certainly certain!" Sadalia said, and she headed down the hall.

With the school day finished, Sadalia headed to her locker and grabbed her books and her backpack. She slung it over her shoulder and walked over to Althea's locker.

"Another day, another disaster," Althea said. "They really piled it on today. I think even my homework has homework."

"In that case, we should totally hang out," Sadalia said.

"I thought you were the responsible one,

Miss Soon-to-Be-Editor-in-Chief," Althea teased.

"Oh, there's no question that I'm the responsible one," Sadalia replied. "But I still think we need to blow off some steam. It's been a weird, weird time."

"I'm sold," Althea said, grabbing her backpack and slamming her locker shut. "My homework's not going anywhere, unfortunately. But we are. Let's do it."

As they walked down the hall, they were joined by Parthenope and Gurge, and the four of them walked toward the front doors of the school.

When they got outside, Sadalia saw Ian standing there with Kagar, waiting for her.

"Hey, you're here!" she said.

"Yeah, why wouldn't I be?" Ian asked. "So are you guys ready to go?"

"What do you mean, 'you guys'?" Sadalia said. "You mean, like . . . all of us?"

"Yeah!" Ian said enthusiastically. "I figured I owe you all anyway, considering my non-party and everything."

Sadalia laughed. "That sounds awesome. What do you all think?"

"Hang out with the guy who defeated a dragon?" Althea said. "Um, yeah!"

Sadalia and her friends joined Ian and Kagar, and the group walked toward Ian's house.

When Ian opened the front door, Blazey was there, leaping right on top of Ian.

"Hey, girl!" Ian said as he introduced his pet dragon to his friends. Blazey licked Ian's face, and he rubbed the dragon's belly.

"Behold!" came a voice from behind the door, and suddenly, Barley was there, leaping into view. He was wearing what looked like armor: he had on a helmet and a metal breastplate that covered his chest. In his hand, he held a sword. "Adventure awaits us all! Will you join me in a campaign of *Quests of Yore?*"

"Is that . . . Barley?" Althea asked. "The guy who climbed the fountain—the one who braved the Path of Peril, and fought the dragon, and got shrunken down to a teeny-tiny size?"

"He is so cool," Gurge said.

Althea nodded and Parthenope gave a big thumbs-up.

"Of course he's cool," Ian said. "He's my brother."

Sadalia smiled. "So let's get questing!" she said as they walked into Ian's living room.

Adventure was waiting!